Seeing Shannon

by

JoMarie DeGioia

PUBLISHED BY

Bailey Park Publishing

ISBN: 978-1-944181-21-5

Seeing Shannon

Book Six of the
Cypress Corners Series

by

JoMarie DeGioia

Chapter 1

Cypress Corners, Florida

"Thanks for coming in today, Bill."

"Thank you, sir." Billy Harris stood and shook Mr. Forbes' offered hand. "I'm eager to get started."

Mr. Forbes, the developer of Cypress Corners, smiled. "Our residents will be eager to hear just what you have planned for that plot out past the town center." He winked. "Not to mention our salespeople."

Billy nodded. "I'll bet."

Billy knew that what he proposed would bring visitors into the property and give residents a fun learning and shopping experience.

"I've arranged a tour with one of our people today, Bill. Jessie is just the person to show you the east side of the property. I'll have her meet you in the lobby."

"Sounds good," Billy said. "I should have preliminary plans within the month."

He managed to walk out of the guy's office without throwing a fist up in triumph. Cypress Corners, an environmentally-conscious and very successful development in Central Florida, was the ideal setting for what he had planned. He had dreams and now, thanks to a recent inheritance, he had the means to see those dreams through.

Stepping up to the desk in the lobby, he smiled at the older woman seated there. "Hi, I'm waiting for a tour Mr. Forbes arranged?" he said.

The woman clicked her fingers on her keyboard. She smiled at him. "Jessie will be out in a sec."

"Thanks," he said.

He refrained from pacing, but it was tough. He couldn't wait to get another look at the plot he'd reserved and, today, the salesperson would see the deal through for him.

Brushing his dark hair out of his eyes, he stared out the wide front windows toward what he knew was the east side of the property.

"Mr. Harris?"

He turned at the sound of the woman's voice, and was stunned when he got a look at her. Damn, he knew she looked like her sister, but seeing the near-twin of the one who got away was like a punch in the chest.

"Billy, please," he said.

"Billy. I'm Jessie." She smiled and then tilted her head, her blond bangs falling to one side of her brow. "Do I know you?"

His face felt hot but he shook his head. "I don't think so."

"Hmm." Her eyes continued to run over him before she seemed to snap out of it. "I have a cart charged and ready to go."

"Great," he said, waving her ahead of him.

They walked past a row of golf carts parked at the curb until they came to one with fat, nubby tires. She slid behind the wheel and he took the seat next to her. He could still feel her eyes on him, but he hoped she wouldn't remember just where she'd seen him. It was true she didn't really know him, but that was because she'd been asleep when he'd fallen into her bed.

She was talking about the amenities of the wilder parts of Cypress as she drove the cart, but he was thinking about that last night he'd spent with her sister, Shannon.

Shannon. They'd had one night together last year, one he'd replayed in his mind a thousand times. Then he'd watched her date jerk after jerk, and had been determined not to fall into that category. On another night three months ago, when he'd fallen into Jessie's bed, he'd had way too many beers. He'd been trying to get up the nerve to tell Shannon what he really felt for her. Jeez, even liquid courage hadn't help him then.

Excitement tingled at the back of his neck as they rounded a curve toward a sandy path. This was it.

"Your plot is just ahead," she said.

Billy sat up straighter in his seat. "Yeah." He could hear the breathlessness in his voice and didn't even try to tamp it down. "Yeah, I see it."

She threw him a smile. "It's a lovely piece of land, Billy."

Billy returned the expression. "Thanks. I can't wait to get started."

Jessie steered the cart to the side of the sandy path and turned off the motor. "Mr. Forbes has only given us a little information."

"Sorry, Jessie. Until I have the property secured, and official plans drawn up, I don't want to say anything." He winked. "I don't want to jinx it."

She blew out a breath before giving a nod. "Yeah, yeah."

Chuckling, he stepped out and crossed over the scrub-covered dirt to reach the edge of his property. Five acres of prime land in Cypress Corners would soon be his. He'd build a house and a store here. And a farm. A goat farm, actually. With a petting zoo and a store to sell goat's-milk soap and other natural products. He just had to get more info on the best way to go about it all.

"You're building a house out here, right?" she asked. "In addition to your farm or ranch thing?"

"Boy, Forbes really hasn't told you guys much of anything has he?"

"I'm sure when your plans are finalized he'll call a meeting. He loves meetings."

He nodded absently. His mind was focused on his land at the moment. At the opportunity it represented. He couldn't screw this up. He had to prove that he was a worthy beneficiary of his late uncle's, and success on this desirable property was a big step in that direction. He'd gone twenty-nine years without any real warmth from the guy. He would take this surprise as the boon it was, and make the absolute most of it.

He'd researched online. He'd gone to a few farms out in St. Cloud to see how to raise and care for the little guys. He'd even talked to some farmers about buying his own stock. There was nothing in the surrounding area that came close to what he wanted to create. There *was* a place in Florida, though. An operation currently under construction southwest of here on the Gulf Coast that would be something he really wanted to emulate. The preliminary plans were exactly what he envisioned for his own piece of paradise, on a larger scale of course.

He'd even made a reservation at the nearby resort for a two-week visit, and would drive down there in the morning. The resort was pretty pricey, but it was an expense he was willing to bear. If he played his cards right, maybe it would be a deductible business expense.

He wouldn't think about the person he'd love to share this all with. The girl he wished he could bring to live on this piece of land. No. Shannon was gone. He had that information from her dick of a last boyfriend, and Billy wasn't going to bring her up to her sister right now. Forbes didn't like to tip his hand? Billy would hold the cards until they cried.

He'd go to Serenity Shores and figure out how to be a success. He'd lost Shannon before he'd even had her. He wouldn't lose this chance, too.

***

Crescent Resort & Spa
Serenity Shores, Crescent Key, Florida

Shannon Wilde straightened her nametag, admiring the brushed golden glow surrounding her name. Her white blouse was crisp and her tan capris pressed. Her hair, now returned to nearly her natural blond and longer than she'd worn it in a long time, was held back with a lacy peach headband.

She was the first person many of their clients saw when they breezed in through the wide, frosted glass doors of Serenity Spa, so she had to look neat and fresh. She might only be a receptionist in the spa at Crescent, but this job was a far cry from slinging beer and hot wings at the End Zone sports bar in St. Cloud. That was for sure. Her old life felt like it was years ago instead of just over a month.

Serenity Shores was lush, and unlike any place she'd ever seen. Even the shoreline, just steps from the resort, was different from what she was used to. Driving forty minutes to the Atlantic every couple of weeks pretty much summed up her beach experience in Central Florida. Serenity Shores, though? Serene waves, crystal clear waters and soft-as-silk sand made this place the popular tourist and wedding destination it was. Now, anyway.

Her boss, spa manager Marion Tucker, had filled her in on what had happened to turn this place from forgotten into unforgettable. This very resort, built a few years ago after a devastating hurricane, changed Crescent Key and the surrounding area into something that attracted the rich and super-rich. In Shannon's initial interview, Mrs. Tucker had instructed her on the particulars of their clientele. Millionaires and vacationers, honeymooners and wedding parties all came to Crescent, and the spa was an integral and desirable part of just about every event that went on here. Again, even the clientele was worlds apart from the rednecks and dude-bros that she used to wait on at the sports bar.

Shannon had left Central Florida with nowhere else to go, really. It had been a visitor to Cypress Corners who had gone on and on about this resort set in a tropical paradise. Crescent was gorgeous, and more popular every day. The service was impeccable, the furnishings luxurious, and the view of Serenity Shores unparalleled. She'd doubted such a paradise was real, but she'd gotten into the Miata her father had bought her ten years earlier on her sixteenth birthday and left St. Cloud, Cypress Corners, and her sister, behind.

A pang of guilt struck her. She and her sister had grown apart after their father died five years ago, and they had only just been starting to reconnect when Shannon had decided she'd had enough. Not of her sister Jessie, of course. Jessie was sweet and a little bit sassy, now that the love of her life had brought her out of her shell. Shannon didn't begrudge her that obvious happiness, but it served to remind her that she would never have that kind of bliss. She was terrible at picking men, and the string of losers she'd given her time and sometimes her heart to weren't worth the energy it took to remember them.

She'd moved to Crescent Key for a reboot, after all. She'd left a trail of mistakes behind her and was ready to start her life over. She was done leading with her heart. Marion was gracious enough to offer a waitress this job, so Shannon was going to focus on the spa and keep her heart to herself.

It was nearly lunch time, and the morning had been pretty busy for a Tuesday in July. Although days of the week didn't seem to matter to most of the spa's clientele. The ultra-rich didn't seem to take time or season into consideration, as far as she'd noticed. Sipping her kale and blueberry smoothie, Shannon tapped on the keyboard to pull up the afternoon's appointments.

An anniversary couple booked a massage together for one o'clock. A bride-to-be scheduled a mud wrap not long after. A group of women, a bunch of alumni from the local high school in Crescent Key, secured an "afternoon of beauty" which would kick off at exactly two. Shannon swiveled in her chair to the gift bags just waiting for the final touches to be added to the schedule of services and samples of some of the products available in the adjacent shop already tucked inside.

When their guests were finished with their visit, they got to choose from a selection of natural beauty and care products from the woven baskets set on the counter behind Shannon's station. Small jars of creams, bottles of scents and special soaps made the choice delightfully difficult.

Lifting one of the rustic yet creamy soaps to her nose, she inhaled a scent of vanilla and lavender. The soaps all bore names related to the resort, like Mimosa Morning, but the names didn't make the choice any easier. Shannon loved all of them.

Closing her eyes, she breathed in deeper. Lavender was supposed to be calming, so she deepened her breathing and drew the scent into her lungs. She felt her heartrate grow even and her spine soften. All of the mistakes, all of the screw-ups, seemed to wash out of her with every exhale. No one here at Crescent knew about the messes she'd left behind. No one would ever find out.

As if from far away she heard the doors slide open. With a touch of regret, she set the soap back with its sisters and swiveled to greet the new arrival. *Whoa.*

A tall man stood near the rack of pamphlets outlining the spa's services, his hands in the front pockets of his khakis. The action pulled the fabric tight against a pretty fine butt, and the light blue linen shirt stretched across a set of broad shoulders. The sleeves of that shirt were rolled up to show off his tanned forearms. Dark brown hair, kind of shaggy like she liked, brushed his collar. Her guy magnet hummed to life and she wished she still held the lavender soap to her nose. If she was attracted to this guy without even seeing his face, he had to be a jerk. Her record would remain unbeaten.

She took in a breath and straightened her shoulders. Channeling her boss, she adopted a serene expression.

"May I help you?" she asked.

He turned his head towards her, his gray-blue eyes opened wide. Her heart tumbled down to her stomach. It was Billy Harris. From St. Cloud.

The one guy who knew all of her dirty secrets.

Crap.

Chapter 2

Billy blinked at the girl behind the counter. It couldn't be. That perfect heart-shaped face, those big golden-brown eyes, those full pink lips. Her hair was different, lighter and longer than he remembered. But it was her. Shannon.

"What the hell?" he mumbled.

"Hello, Billy," she said in a soft voice.

Her brows were drawn together and, unless he missed his guess, she looked worried.

"You're down here?" He gave a shake of his head. "You're in Serenity Shores?"

She nodded, straightening in her chair. She was a little thing, but even her pressed work clothes couldn't hide the lush curves he knew she had.

"I work here at Serenity." Her tone was clipped and very un-Shannon. "May I help you with something today?"

"I…" Why had he come to the spa? Oh, yeah. Soap. "I was told the spa carries the goat's-milk soaps made by Jo Potter."

"We do." There was a touch of pride in her voice. "What scent would you like?"

"I have no clue." He felt a smile curve his lips. "I'm just

getting into this. Maybe you can make a suggestion?"

She bit her bottom lip, he sure loved that bottom lip of hers, and shrugged. "Do you want to relax? Be energized? Soothed?"

He chuckled. "How about clean?"

She smiled a little bit, the first sign of a crack in her armor. "Almond. Clean and a little bit warm." She turned toward the low shelf behind her desk and grabbed a chucky rectangle about the size of her palm and held it out to him. "Here you go."

He took it, his fingers brushing over her hand. That electricity he'd always felt just being around her sparked to life. *Great.*

"Thanks." The bar was surprisingly light for its size, and he brought it to his nose to give it a sniff. "It smells creamy, if that's possible."

"It's something about the goat's milk."

He held on to the soap and reached into his back pocket with his free hand. "How much is it?"

She shook her head, her silky hair brushing her shoulders. "We don't sell it here. The shop is through that archway."

"Okay." He put the soap on the counter. "I'll have to pick up a couple of bars."

She stared at him, that look of worry etched on her face once more. "Why are you here?"

"Research, mostly. For my business."

"Your business?" One fair brow arched up toward her headband. "What, your uncle is opening a spa?"

He barked out a laugh. "Imagine that? Wild Harry Harris, running a spa."

"Then, what?"

"I'm starting a farm, Shannon. A goat farm, actually."

She blinked at him. "Goats?" Then she laughed, a light musical laugh he'd rarely heard from her before. "You. And goats?"

"What's so funny?"

Holding up a hand, she pursed her lips and shook her head. Her eyes danced, though. Her cheeks were pink and she was obviously keeping something back.

"Shannon," he drawled. "Come on. What's so funny about me and goats?"

She blew out a breath and grinned. "Billy Goat. Seriously? That's too funny."

A smile tugged at his lips. "All right, I'll give you that one."

She folded her arms on the counter, tilting her head to the side. "If you ask in the shop, they'll give you more info on the farm. It's small right now."

"Yep. I've seen the plans online, though. From the announcement a few months back. The farm, the house, the tourist center they're going to build next to the soccer complex."

"Is that what you're going to build?" At his nod, she went on. "Where? In St. Cloud?"

"No. Cypress Corners."

Her brow furrowed again.

"That will be nice," she said in a flat voice. She bit that lip again, and then her gaze slid to her computer. "I have to get back to work."

He hadn't dreamed of running into her but he didn't want their conversation to end. Damn it, they used to be able to talk. Over a couple of beers, on more than one occasion, he'd told her more than he'd ever told anyone. About his fucked-up family situation. About his desire to be more than a hired hand on his uncle's farm. And he knew how she'd felt after her father died and she began to lose a connection to her sister. He'd commiserated. He was an only child, orphaned and raised by his wild-man uncle.

"I'm staying here for a couple of weeks," he told her.

"Where?" She faced him again. "Here?"

"At Crescent."

Her mouth dropped open. "Why?"

Leaning against the counter, his elbow close to her arm, he shrugged. "I want to learn as much as I can. Start off on the right foot, and all."

"Oh." She sank back in her chair. "Enjoy your stay."

Brr. That was ice cold. Shannon Wilde was a lot of things in his memory, but she was never cold.

He rubbed the back of his neck, gearing up to take another stab at it. "Want to grab a drink later? After work?"

A quick shake of her head sent that idea into the crapper. "No, thanks. Hey, it was really nice to see you though."

He stiffened. *And...the brush-off.* "Yeah, you too. See you around."

He turned from her and went into the frou-frou spa shop to look at more soaps. Sure, he hadn't spoken to her since that night in March. She'd moved in with her latest ass-hat and he'd tried to move on in his own turn. That moment when she'd laughed at him, that had felt familiar. Real. Like he was seeing the Shannon he knew she was deep down. The girl he'd held in his arms six months ago. Then he'd mentioned Cypress Corners. Maybe she was still estranged from her sister. That might explain the icy wind that had blown over him and chilled his balls.

He guessed she knew what plots of land went for in Cypress. Her sister was one of their top salespeople, after all. He'd only been a good ol' boy in a pickup truck when they'd…not dated, actually. When they'd hung out after their first and only hook-up. With the same bunch of people from the End Zone and never alone again. Until that night he'd missed his opportunity. What did she think now? That he had money to spend? Or that he was still working for his uncle and getting paid in room and board?

"May I help you?" a girl asked him, echoing Shannon's greeting in the spa.

He nodded at the pretty redhead working the counter. "I'd like to buy some goat's-milk soaps."

She girl smiled and led him to a display stacked with

soaps tied with bits of straw. There seemed to be a lot of different ones to choose from, in just about every soft color he could imagine.

"What kind would you like?" she asked him.

He finally found a smile. "How about one of each?"

***

"It's five o'clock," Marion said, breezing in from her office to the spa reception area.

"I know." Shannon turned to face her boss. "I'm just checking tomorrow's schedule of appointments."

"Wednesday is usually light, but there are two weddings booked for this weekend," Marion said. "Not so light tomorrow, huh?"

"No. Guests and the wedding parties are starting to arrive. I went ahead and called in the reinforcements. Kayla's booked solid."

Marion smiled. "Great. We can certainly use them."

They kept a list of manicurists, massage therapists and other spa technicians who were available to fill in or, in this case to pitch in, at the spa. Kayla, their best massage therapist, would literally have her hands full this week. The reputation of Serenity was such that it was never difficult finding someone who wanted to work there, even on a temporary basis. Shannon was beginning to get the feel for the ebb and flow of the business, though the tide seemed to be on the way in more often than on the way out.

"Now go home," her boss said.

"Will do. Have a nice night."

"You too."

Marion headed back to her office, no doubt to finish up whatever business she had left to do. Shannon clicked off her computer and grabbed her bag from a drawer set in the bottom of the counter. As she straightened, her gaze fell on the bar of almond soap Billy had left behind. Lifting it to her nose, she breathed in. Mmm.

So Billy was here in Serenity Shores. So what? That didn't have to mean anything. He was doing research for his business. A goat farm, of all things. He was staying here for two weeks, though. In the resort. Just across the lobby from where she worked.

The heels of her flats clicked dully over the tile floor as she made her way through the lobby. Keeping her eyes focused straight ahead, she avoided any glimpse of Billy should he be among the guests milling about. She'd worked hard to prove herself to Marion, and it seemed like the woman was pleased with Shannon's work. The spa was a dream spot, and she counted herself very lucky to have landed this job. Would that change, though? What if her boss learned what a screw-up Shannon had been before? That her taste and judgment in all things male led her to do the dumbest things. And then there was Billy.

He was one guy who didn't seem to fit in with her usual bunch of dude-bros, but after they'd slept together he'd put her straight into the friend zone where she'd been happy to stay. Back then, anyway.

He was always sweet. Quiet most of the time, when his loud buddies were around. They'd talked sometimes, though. Talked and shared things she'd never divulged to anyone else. He never pushed her for more, either. The pull was still there. The attraction she'd felt from the first time she met him. But she'd never been very smart about the physical side of things. Give her pretty eyes and a broad set of shoulders and she was set. Hadn't she thrown in with Rob-the-dick because of just those things?

A twinge high on her left cheekbone, a phantom memory of pain and embarrassment, reminded her of just what had been the last straw in that relationship. A punch to the face was enough to set a girl straight, wasn't it? It was for this girl.

She unlocked her little Miata and slid behind the wheel. Almost ten years later, she still loved the thing. It reminded her of her dad, a serious academic who had a wild streak that only seemed to come out around her. Yes, he might have shared a love of books and the environment with her sister Jessie but Shannon was the one who went to Old Town Village and rode the zip line with him. She was the one who took off to the beach on the east coast with him and their boogie boards. When she looked out at the gentle waves of Serenity Shores she could almost see him clutching his board with his skinny arms, a big broad grin on his face.

Tossing her bag on the passenger seat, she started the car and drove to her rented rooms over near the Crisscross motel. There wasn't a lot to Crescent Key in the way of accommodations in her budget, and finding the small efficiency set just off of Main Street had been all her boss's doing. It seemed that the older couple who owned the house took Marion's word regarding Shannon's reliability too, and happily rented her the second floor walk-up. Steep walk-up, actually.

Crooked stairs that clung to the back of the narrow old house just to the side of the Bilco doors to the basement. Clotheslines stretched from the back of the frame home to a metal T in the backyard. When the breeze kicked up, the metal clothesline wheels pinged and creaked, but the sounds were soothing when Shannon had trouble falling asleep in the double bed in her little bedroom.

She turned off of Shore Drive onto Main Street. This spot where the roads crossed paths, she'd been told repeatedly, was the historic site of first traffic light on the island. Crescent Key was an even smaller town than St. Cloud, and it had a very different vibe. No rednecks flying their Confederate flags off the back of their raised pickup trucks. No ranch hands hitting on her at work.

There were a few similarities, though. The hokey convenience store owned and operated by a nosy old lady would fit right in on the main street in downtown St. Cloud. The pointed glares the woman gave Shannon whenever she went in there was enough to keep those visits quick and quiet. For God's sake, she'd had enough of gossip back home. Enough of everyone knowing about her latest hook-up or latest mistake. And boy, had there been a lot of them.

She let herself into her cozy little apartment and kicked off her shoes. The place was small but neat as a pin. Despite telling her landlady over and over again that she didn't have to look after Shannon, Mrs. Battle still snuck in here and tidied. Shannon couldn't be mad about that. It was so nice to come home to a clean place, and both the woman and her husband were as sweet as anybody Shannon had ever known.

Her apartment looked like a time capsule, though. Big, soft floral couch. Walnut furniture polished to a high sheen. Chrome-trimmed Formica table flanked by four chairs with sparkly vinyl seats. It was probably what her sister Jessie would call "retro-chic" and Shannon was starting to like it.

She grabbed a bottle of juice out of the curved fifties refrigerator and settled on the couch. She'd fallen asleep there last night, watching an old sitcom on the seriously-retro but perfectly fine TV. It was a console, and actually had a record player tucked down into the top of it. More polished walnut wood there, too. And since the super-soft pink afghan blanket was folded neatly over the back of the couch, it was clear Mrs. Battle had struck again.

Shannon didn't turn the TV on. Nope. She sipped her

blueberry-pomegranate juice and thought about the life she'd left behind. The guys she'd tossed her heart, and body, at without a thought. But more than that?

She thought about Billy.

Billy had seemed so different from the other guys she'd been with when she'd first met him. And he was. Their one night together was hot and tender, and had scared her from daring to hope that they could be an item. He'd seemed as relieved as she had been to slide into the friend zone, so she'd just talked to him whenever they found themselves relatively alone. About anything and everything.

Billy was a sweet guy. With a killer smile and a body she could still envision when she shut her eyes. He'd been out of her league six months ago. Kind and hot and…nice. That was the reason she'd pushed him away. She had no clue about what to do with a nice guy.

Now that he was starting his own business? It was clear he'd come into some money from somewhere. His clothes were neat and fit his big body really well. He looked expensive. So add money to mix, and he was a guy who could have any girl he wanted.

So why would he ever want her?

Chapter 3

Billy shifted on his barstool, turning to face the incredible view toward the bay. In July sunset was just about as late as it got, and the sky at five o'clock was still as bright as midday. Electric blue dotted with puffy white clouds that were reflected in the nearly-still water. He could see why Crescent Resort and Spa was so successful. Eye-catching architecture, smooth lines and jewel-toned accents combined to create a place people would gladly come to again and again.

After his run-in with Shannon, he'd put his things in his incredibly-plush guest room and then gotten the hell out of there. Even in crisp khakis and a button-down oxford shirt, clothes that cost more than he'd ever spent on them up until a month ago, he still felt like the poor relation. Looking around the Victorian-inspired resort, with its fancy trimmings and sharp attention to a guest's every comfort, his chest began to itch. He couldn't shake the feeling that he didn't belong here.

Sipping his drink, something with rum and lime that the bartender had informed him was the drink of the day, he thought about his next move. He'd sent Jo Potter an email when he'd been back in St. Cloud, and they had a meeting scheduled for Friday afternoon. That gave him three days to sit and chill before he took the next step in his master plan.

Billy would head out to her little farm, as it was currently, and get her input on just what he should do with his own piece of property. Even though the new facility was months away from opening, she was gracious enough to offer to share with him what she knew of the kids and does and bucks. What she knew was pretty extensive. He was eager to see the little buggers, too.

Working as a vet's assistant in St. Cloud had helped him get into the University of Florida, where he'd gotten his undergrad in Animal Science, but his work on his uncle's ranch had given him a more practical place to apply what he'd learned. Tuition had come at a steep price, though. He'd worked for room and board and tuition for four long years. Six years after graduation, he'd still felt like he could never pay the man back. That was, until his uncle died and left a boatload of money to Billy. The ranch? That went to his cousins as it should.

He drained his drink, and the ice clinked softly as he set the glass back on the polished-wood bar.

"Another one?" the girl behind the bar asked him.

"No, thanks. Hey, can I get something to eat?"

The bartender nodded. "Burgers. Bar food." She shrugged, tossing her dark ponytail back over her shoulder. "You know."

"Sounds pretty good right now. I'll have a burger, medium rare, with fries."

She leaned on the bar, angling her upper body toward him. "So, no reservations at Wisteria? That's a shame."

He looked down the V of her shirt at some pretty impressive and probably enhanced cleavage, he was a guy after all, and then met her eyes. "Not really my speed."

"You know, I could probably snag you a reservation." She smiled now, tilting her head to one side. "Maybe a dinner partner, too."

He deflected her flirting with a smile. "No thanks. Just the burger tonight."

After a beat she walked away to put in Billy's order. Wisteria. Reservations were in high demand at the place, or so the guy at the check-in desk had insisted. Billy hadn't given the fancy restaurant a second glance as he'd walked through the lobby. It wasn't really his kind of place.

He watched the bartender flirt with a couple of guys

down the other end of the bar and wished for a second that he'd wanted to take her up on her offer. Not just for dinner, either. Maybe dinner would lead to drinks, which would lead to trying out that huge jetted tub in his guest room. And just maybe he wouldn't be sitting here all night thinking about Shannon.

Shannon looked good. Really good. Confident like he'd never seen her before. She looked fantastic with those loose waves in her hair. Soft and so pretty. He'd known she was a natural blond despite the inky-black dye she used to wear, not that he was going to remind her just how he knew that. He'd only asked her to join him for a drink, and she'd turned him down just as easily as she'd shoved him into the friend zone six months ago. He had to admit, that stung like a bitch.

Was she seeing someone in Serenity Shores? The possibility twisted his gut. It shouldn't. He had no claim there, other than his long-time crush on her. He'd relived their night together over and over again. Not the one he'd wasted but the one when he'd gotten into her bed. He couldn't remember a time, before or since, when he'd felt heat like that. They'd scratched each other's itch, of course. That night they couldn't get each other's clothes off fast enough. She'd made the sweetest sounds as he'd driven her out of her mind. She'd turned him inside out, too. Her hands. Her mouth. Her… *Damn.*

Rubbing his hand over his face, he growled.

"Easy, big guy." The bartender was back with his food. "Here's your burger."

"Thanks."

She lingered but he just tucked into his food until she slid away from him. Six months. That was a long time to spend thinking about the one that got away. She'd moved on, hadn't she? Hell, he had too. One-night stands and drunken hook-ups hadn't come close to that night with Shannon, though.

"Hey, you're the soap guy," someone said to his right.

Turning his head, he saw it was the pretty redhead from the spa shop. He swallowed the bite of burger in his mouth. "Yeah, I guess so. I'm Billy Harris."

"Hi, Billy Harris. I'm Carrie." She perched on the stool next to him, crossing her ankles. She wore an outfit like Shannon had, and she looked just as neat and pressed in the white shirt and tan pants. Her hair was pulled back like Shannon's too.

"Hi, Carrie."

"So, what's with all the soap?" she asked.

"Research."

She blinked. "Research?"

"I'm starting a goat farm. Soap. Milk. Cheese."

Her blue eyes widened. ""Like the one they're going to build out near the Serenity Shores Sand Dollars soccer complex?"

Billy smiled. "Not that big, but yes. I have some property up in Central Florida, so I'm down here to get some pointers."

"Goats." She bit her lip, and then chuckled. "Billy, huh?"

He knew what was coming. "Yep."

She laughed out loud now. "Billy Goat."

He rolled his eyes but quirked a smile. "So I've heard."

"Sorry. It was just so obvious, you know?" She jumped and stared at the phone in her hand. "That's my guy. Gotta run. Good luck with your farm, Billy Goat."

He didn't even try to fight it as she hopped down from the stool and ran toward a guy waving from the entrance. He just went back to his burger.

Billy Goat. He supposed it wasn't so bad as far as nicknames went. He'd certainly had worse growing up. Misfit. Orphan. Suck-up. He wondered what his cousins thought about him now that their father had left him over half a million dollars. Did they think his sucking-up had been for the money he hadn't even known Wild Harry Harris was packing? Let them. He'd been as surprised as any of them.

It struck him that he had two weeks to spend in a slice of paradise on the Gulf. He would learn what he needed to for the farm, of course. But that left him more than enough time to play.

Shannon was here, too. Yeah, she was working but she had to have some free time, right? She wanted to keep him in the friggin' friend zone, huh? What was wrong with a friend taking another friend out to lunch? Nothing he could think of. If she wanted him to see her as a friend, he could do that. For now.

"What are you smiling about, Billy Goat?" the bartender asked, sliding his check toward him on the bar.

He glanced up at her. "Heard that, did you?"

She smiled. "I think it's cute."

Shrugging, he grabbed the pen and signed his name and

room number. "Charge this to my room?"

"Sure."

Before she could start up with the flirting again, he stood and headed back inside. There had to be a reason Shannon was here. It couldn't be a coincidence. Dumb luck, maybe. His smile widened. If there was one thing he'd learned at Harry's knee, it was to never look a gift horse in the mouth.

***

Shannon felt a little less frantic this morning than she had last night. Even a quiet evening at home hadn't had its usual calming effect on her. Thoughts of Billy kept intruding. Billy as he'd made love to her six months ago. Billy as the friend he'd been back in St. Cloud. Billy as the guy who could blow away what she was starting to build here with just one word.

When she thought about all the mistakes she'd made, and how Billy had a ring-side seat for all of them, shame crawled up the back of her neck. Squaring her shoulders, she breezed through the doors of the spa and settled herself behind the counter and started her day.

Taking a long sip of the café latte she'd picked up on

the way in helped to wash a little bit of the bitterness out of her mouth. God, she was such an idiot. She'd been smart to turn down Billy's offer for drinks. There was no question about that. Now if she could just get him out of her head.

"Morning, Shannon," Carrie from the spa shop said as she came in from the lobby. "How was your night?"

"Okay. Yours?"

Carrie's eyes sparkled. "Great. I met up with my guy for drinks at the pool-side bar."

Shannon just nodded.

"Oh!" Carrie went on. "I ran into that tall, dark and handsome guy from the shop."

Shannon's heart tripped. "Who?" As if she didn't know.

"The goat guy." Carrie laughed lightly. "Billy Goat."

Shannon smiled. "That's what I called him yesterday."

"He bought one of every kind of goat's-milk soap we carry." Carrie pursed her lips. "He doesn't seem like a goatherd, right?"

"You can't picture him in lederhosen?"

"No. He looks more like a hot cowboy."

Yeah, he was. "He was raised on a ranch."

Shannon knew her mistake immediately when Carrie's

brows shot up to her hairline.

"You know him? Like, from before?"

Before. Before being pre-Crescent, no doubt. It seemed that Shannon wasn't the only one who thought of this place as a new beginning. Carrie probably had a story, too. Didn't everybody? She doubted the pretty redhead had as many skeletons in her closet as she did.

"Yes," Shannon said.

Carrie sighed. "He's dreamy. Did you two used to go out?"

"No," Shannon said truthfully.

Carrie clicked her tongue. "That's a shame. That smile, those eyes." She winked. "Those shoulders."

"Taking inventory, Carrie?" Marion asked with a smile as she joined them.

Carrie started. "Just talking about Shannon's old flame."

"He's not my old flame." Shannon's denial sounded weak to her own ears. "We used to know each other. That's all."

Marion gave a slow nod. "Be careful, Shannon. There's a certain custom here in Serenity Shores."

Shannon blinked. "A custom?"

"Yes. Toes in the sand, heart in your hand. Trust me, it happened to me."

Carrie giggled. "Me, too."

Shannon shook her head. "My shoes are staying on, thanks. No sand on these toes." She turned in her chair and held her legs straight out. Her pretty pink flats were snug on her feet. "See?"

Carrie and Marion exchanged a look that Shannon chose to ignore.

"Just saying." Then Marion clapped her hands together. "We're going to be swamped today, ladies. So let's get ready!"

Carrie turned and hurried back into the shop while Shannon pulled up the day's schedule.

"Hey, Shannon," her boss said, her voice lowered.

Shannon gave Marion her full attention. "Yes?"

"It can be fun, you know. Giving someone your heart. Falling in love."

"I've fallen before," Shannon said. "I don't ever want to fall again."

Concern darkened Marion's big brown eyes. "There's a story there."

40

"Maybe. But it's not one I'm going to tell." Shannon held up one hand. "Trust me, it's not a nice one."

Marion's smile was full of compassion, and Shannon's eyes pricked with tears.

"Hop to it, then," Marion said, her voice upbeat once more.

Shannon dipped her head and returned her attention to the computer screen. By the time they opened for business she had no time to think about falling. The morning went by in a rush and when lunch time rolled around, she was starving.

"We're closing up shop, Shannon," Carrie said. "Marion said to take an hour to recharge before the afternoon."

Shannon nodded and clicked through her screens to put everything to sleep for now. Looking down, she saw that she had kicked her shoes off while she'd worked. Thankfully Carrie didn't spot them under Shannon's desk.

"Hey there, Billy Goat," Carrie said.

Shannon's heart gave a flip and she closed her eyes. "Why?" she murmured.

Taking a breath, she looked up at him. Oh, he looked

good in a relaxed polo shirt nearly the same color as his eyes and cargo shorts that hung just right off of his hips. He wore Vans sneakers and looked very resort-casual. His hair was brushed back, but still just this side of shaggy. His sculpted lips were in a half-smile and his eyes were bright.

"Hey, Shannon," he said.

"Hey, Billy," she said.

They stared at each other for a long minute, until Carrie coughed.

"Okay, I'll see you after lunch," Carrie said, breezing out the doors into the safety of the lobby.

Shannon watched her go, and then faced Billy again.

"We're closed," she said.

"Oh?"

"For lunch."

His smile grew. "Good. That's why I'm here."

"What?"

"To see if you wanted to grab lunch with me."

She bit her lip. "Oh, Billy I don't know if that's a good idea."

"If what's a good idea?" He came closer and she could smell his hot, fresh scent. "Two friends having lunch?"

"Friends," she repeated.

"Yeah. I thought we were friends."

"We are."

He cocked a brow at her. "So?"

"Okay, lunch."

The smile he flashed her was bright. "Cool."

She slipped her shoes back on, she was so not kicking them off again, and grabbed her bag. "Where to? I only have an hour."

"How about the pool-side bar? I know it's hot out but we could find some shade."

Anyone born and raised in Florida knew the value of chasing shade. The perfect parking spot? Not the one closest to the store. The one in the shade.

"Okay," she said.

He waved her ahead of him and she brushed past, just touching his arm as she did so. A flash of something struck her but she chose to ignore it. She could do this. She could have lunch with an old friend. They were friends. Friends who had seen each other naked once, but still.

She would just get through this hour and then she would know she could resist the urge to throw herself at the closest hot guy.

Chapter 4

Billy kept close to Shannon as they walked out into the sun-drenched pool-side bar. "The burgers here are good."

"They are," she said.

"You've eaten here before?" He lowered his head and looked at her from beneath his brows. "Of course, you have. How long have you been down here?"

"Just over a month."

He thought about that as they reached the makeshift hostess stand at the end of the bar. "Two for lunch."

The hostess smiled and led them over to a table shaded by the three-story edifice behind them. Come late afternoon you'd probably be able to fry an egg on the decking but right now the sun was still just over the resort's main building.

Shannon studied her menu and Billy studied her. She looked fresh and sweet today, like yesterday. He liked seeing her like this. She did look a lot like her sister. But if Jessie looked like a Pixie, Shannon looked like a Nymph or something. Natural. Gorgeous. Hotter than the sun on the sand.

"I ate here last night," he said.

"So you *are* staying here at the resort."

"Yep. Killer room facing the Gulf. There's a view from the bathtub, believe it or not."

Her full lips curved up at one corner. "Took a bubble bath, did you?"

He chuckled. "Not going to do that by myself, thanks. I'd have to hand in my man card."

"I don't know. Carrie said you bought up all the soap she had. Seems you'd be able to work up a nice lather."

Their eyes met like they had in the spa's reception area, and an image of her tangle up and soapy with him in that big tub filled his head. Shifting, he eased the growing pressure in his shorts and forced himself to focus on the menu.

"What do you recommend?" he asked, if only to have something to say.

"Hmm. The crab cakes."

A server came over and poured them each a glass of water. "Have you decided?" he asked.

"I'll have the crab cakes," Shannon said.

"Make that two orders." Billy handed their menus to the server and waited for him to leave them. "How do you like it here?"

Shannon gave him an easy smile. "I like it a lot,

actually."

"I bet it beats working at the End Zone and sharing an apartment with your sister."

Her smile dimmed a little bit.

"Shit, I'm sorry," he said. "I know it's a sore subject."

"You also know who I was recently living with, Billy."

Yeah, Billy knew. Rob-the-dick, her old boss.

"Everybody makes mistakes," he said, keeping his tone light.

She shook her head. "I major in mistakes."

"Not from where I'm sitting."

Her brow furrowed. "Oh?"

He folded his arms and leaned toward her. "You have a great job which you obviously love, and you get to drink in this fantastic view every day. See? No mistakes there."

Her amber eyes were warm. "I'd forgotten that about you."

"Forgotten what?"

"How good you can make me feel."

Her words sent a jolt straight to his groin. "Shannon."

She held up one hand. "That's not what I meant." Covering her eyes, she groaned. "Jeez."

"Hey, don't sweat it," he said. "Friends can talk about anything, right? Even the past?"

She lowered her hand to gaze at him, hope clear on her beautiful face. "I guess so."

"Then let's talk about goats."

That got him the laugh he wanted.

Their lunches came and they talked about his plans for the farm. He wanted to prove himself worthy to Harry's memory, not that his cousins would give a shit. He didn't share that little bit of angst, though. It was early in the day for family drama.

As their hour was nearly up, he sat back. "So how about dinner?"

She smirked at him. "We just had lunch."

"I meant tonight, wise ass."

She laughed now, a light sound. "I guess we could."

"Yeah?"

"Friends eat dinner together, Billy."

He grinned. This was starting to feel good. Familiar. "So, where? Everybody's been talking about Wisteria."

She gave a quick shake of her head. "No way. That's not a friends-going-to-dinner type of place."

No, it wasn't. It was upscale and fancy. Had she gone there on a date? Damn, he hoped not.

"You've eaten there?" he asked.

"Way above my pay grade, Billy Goat."

"Billy Goat." He shook his head. "I'm glad that's catching on. So where do you want to eat?"

"There's a little Mexican place in town. Rancho Casa."

"Great. Does seven sound good?"

She came to her feet as he did. "Sure."

He walked her back to the spa and left her at her desk. That redhead, Carrie, was waiting there for her. Her eyes were bright as she grinned and gave him a wriggling finger wave.

Billy lifted his chin to her, and then faced Shannon. "I thought I'd offer to pick you up tonight, but that might make you feel too date-y."

She nodded her agreement, which he'd known she would.

"So I'll see you there?" he asked.

Shannon bit her lip and thought for a second. "I better meet you here and drive over with you."

"Yeah?"

"It's very popular." She smiled. "No set menu, too."

He raised his brows. "Then the food's gotta be good."

"Oh, it is."

He held up a hand. "Then I'll see you later."

Shannon's cheeks turned a little pink. He walked through the lobby, his mind working. He had a date with Shannon tonight, no matter how he might have framed it. That stuff about meeting her there? That had been purely for her benefit. He was going to get her to see him as something more than a past mistake. As more than a one-night, not to be repeated, fling. He just had to figure this thing out.

He had to be careful. To step lightly if he had any hope of getting out of the friend zone.

***

Shannon stood in front of her closet, picking through the meager collection of clothes she'd brought with her when she'd started this new chapter of her life. White capris and an apricot peasant blouse would work. She dug her cork-heeled wedge sandals out of the closet and slipped them on, making herself at least a teeny bit taller. She'd hardly worn clothes like these when she'd lived in St. Cloud. Yoga pants and T-shirts when she wasn't working and a tight End Zone uniform when she was.

The few weeks she'd spent in Cypress Corners with her sister Jessie had given her a tantalizing taste of small-town life that she hadn't dared to hope to fit. It had also given her the opportunity to wear prettier clothes that felt more like her. Jessie had become really good at searching out bargains up at the outlets in Orlando, and Shannon's trips there had allowed her to buy some nice things without breaking her meager bank.

The afternoon had been very busy at the spa, which had served to keep Carrie out of her face anyway. The girl had smirked so hard after Billy left the spa Shannon had nearly flipped her off. She'd refrained, though. That was how the old Shannon would have responded. Besides, Carrie wasn't a pain in the butt. She just seemed to see something where there was nothing, at least regarding Shannon and Billy.

She refreshed her makeup and ran a brush through her hair. What did Billy think about her new look? It was very different from how she'd been back when they hooked up. She cringed when she thought about that jet black dye job she used to sport. The heavy eye makeup and the sleazy clothes were a part of her past life, too.

Billy had looked her over several times during their lunch, his lips curved in a small smile. She could admit to herself that she looked good, even in her spa uniform. Heaven knew she felt good. Better than she had in years. No more late nights working or partying meant a more-balanced life. She was starting to believe that, anyway. Now she just had to get through this dinner with her "friend."

She drove back to Crescent and found Billy waiting for her in the lobby. He didn't see her at first. His back was to her. His very fine backside, too. His hair looked a little damp, and his clothes were very nice. He wore gray linen trousers that looked soft and hung just right off his narrow hips. His white shirt looked fine and fit his broad shoulders well. He wore oxfords on his feet. Honest to goodness shoes instead of the work boots she'd always seen him wear before this afternoon's sneakers.

"Billy," she said, approaching him.

He glanced over his shoulder, his brows raised. Then he smiled and she felt the tiled floor dip beneath her wedges.

"Shannon."

Oh, the way he said her name. Had he always been so sexy? Their one night together had been amazing, but otherwise he'd been cute and sweet and…comfortable. This guy? Gorgeous and put together?

His eyes ran over her from head to toe, his gaze hot. "You look good."

She brushed her hair back and lifted her chin. "Back atcha." He chuckled and he was Billy again. Brushing aside the conflict between hot sex god and sweet good ol' boy, she smiled brightly at him. "Ready for some killer Mexican food?"

"Oh, yeah. Okay if I drive?"

She nodded and, after waving her ahead of him, they went back outside toward guest parking. To her surprise he wasn't driving his dusty pickup truck here in Serenity Shores. No. The shiny burgundy SUV suited him, though.

"Is this a rental?" she asked as he pressed the fob to unlock her door.

"Nope. It's all mine."

She slid inside, her hands caressing the tan leather seat. "It's nice."

"Thanks. I guess I needed an upgrade from the shit kickin' ride I used to drive everywhere, right?"

Shannon shrugged. "It wasn't that bad, Billy."

He tilted a smile and gave his head a shake. "It was, but that's okay. I still have that truck, by the way. I'll need it for my work on the farm."

"A farm," she marveled out loud. "Your own farm?"

He continued to face forward but she saw the curve of his cheek as he smiled. "Yep."

She wanted to ask him so much more. How was it that he was buying his own place? What had happened since they'd lost touch? None of that was her business, though. They were one-time lovers and reconnected friends now.

She directed him to Rancho Casa and he parked in the small, crowded lot adjacent. Turning off the ignition, Billy peered through the windshield at the nondescript building. The windows facing the street were dimly lit, and you could just make out silhouettes of people inside. She smiled to herself. His reaction was just like hers had been the first time she'd come here with Marion.

"Sure looks busy."

"Trust me, Billy. Prepare to have your mind blown."

His eyes widened a notch. "I'll take your word for it."

They went inside and found the place bustling and busy. The smiling woman standing near the door had no menus to give them. There was a big board with specials written on it, which Billy studied.

"Damn," he said. "Everything sounds good."

She winked at him. "And you haven't seen how many different kinds of Tequilas they serve."

He threw her a smile. "Challenge accepted. Lead on, friend."

Chapter 5

"So tell me about this goat farm," Shannon said.

Billy folded his hands on the table. They'd just ordered a little bit of everything off the specials board, *tamales, chiles rellenos* and *carne asada*. He'd been raised on a ranch, and couldn't resist the lure of beef no matter how delicious everything else sounded. She was sipping a margarita from a glass the size of her face while he was drinking an ice cold Corona beer.

"What do you want to know?"

She leaned a little bit forward and he was struck again by how gorgeous she looked. The thin gauzy pink top she wore hugged her breasts and her hair caught the light from the hanging fixture above their table. They were seated at a small round table for two, and the setting was intimate despite the surrounding diners.

"You're going to build in Cypress?" she asked.

"Yep. Bought a five-acre plot of land east of the town center."

Her brow furrowed. "Why there? Why not in St. Cloud?"

He smirked at her. "You and I both grew up in St.

Cloud, Shannon. Do you think it's ready for a shop selling goats' milk, cheese and soaps?"

She laughed, that light sound he loved. "I guess not."

He fingered the neck of his beer bottle. "Besides I want something that's just mine, you know?"

It was a revelation, as far as he was concerned anyway. She might know, like everybody in their hometown did, that he'd been taken in by his uncle's family when his own parents died. What nobody knew was how he'd always felt like an outsider. Like nothing was truly his.

"I get that."

He supposed she did. Both she and her sister had been lost when their father died, or so Shannon had told him on one night they'd spent talking. Jessie found her place, her life, in Cypress but Shannon had stayed in St. Cloud with her circle of asshole friends who only seemed to look out for themselves.

She took another sip of her drink, letting a little sound of delight. "Oh, that's good."

"And potent, from the smell of it."

"Worried about me, Billy Goat?"

"I'm driving, so not really. Plus you're usually the one

to keep her head."

"Most of the time."

Her gaze skittered away and he wondered what she was thinking about. Drunken hookups? He could commiserate there. Falling into toxic relationships? He had no clue about that since he'd never had a serious relationship, toxic or otherwise.

"Tell me about how you came to work at Crescent," he asked.

As he'd hoped, she brightened at the change of subject.

"Jessie was touring a group at Cypress, and they couldn't stop talking about the resort. I'd joined them for dinner after, and totally bought into what they were saying. When the woman offered to talk to Marion Tucker about a job for me, I thought she was just being nice. Imagine my surprise when I got the call saying I had an interview!"

"You came down here on the strength of an interview?" He gave a slow nod. "Impressive."

She splayed her hands on the table. "I had nothing to lose. What did I have to keep me up there?"

Me. He took another swig of his beer. He wasn't anyone to stick around for, apparently. The blame for that fell squarely on his shoulders. He'd let her push him away after their first night together and when he'd had a chance to tell her how he felt? He'd fucked it up.

"It seems to have worked out for you," he said.

Her mouth fell open and he worried that she'd heard something in his voice. A need to be more than himself to at least one person other than his late uncle. It was a shame that Wild Harry Harris never let Billy know how he felt about him until he was dead and gone.

Before he could embarrass himself, the food was served. Steam filled with spice surrounded them, so they dug in.

After a few minutes, Shannon gave a short laugh. He eyed her, seeing the humor dancing in her expression.

"What?" he asked as he unwrapped his second *tamale*.

"You like it, I take it?"

Groaning, he grinned at her. "You weren't kidding."

She cut into a big fat *chimichanga*, letting out a groan of her own as she swallowed a bite. "Mmm."

"I thought you were a regular here."

She licked her lips, which drew his eye to her delectable mouth. "I've only been here a couple of times, but it's never disappointed me."

He took a bite of the tender *tamale* filling and nearly said a prayer. "I'm glad you suggested it."

She smiled and they each drained their drinks. He ordered another round and almost before he was ready it looked like their date was over. Their plates were empty and their drinks nearly so. He settled the bill and they climbed back into his SUV.

Her scent was strong here, with the windows rolled up. The closeness of the space, and the heat from Shannon's body, was starting to make him hard so he started the engine to at least have the A/C cool him a little.

"This was fun," she said. Her cheeks were pink and her eyes bright. "Thanks for being so pushy."

He arched a brow at her. "I might be a little bull-headed, but nobody's ever called me pushy."

She shrugged, causing her pretty shirt to slip off one smooth-looking shoulder. "No. You're nice. Sweet."

"Sweet?" He let her see the heat in his eyes. "That's another first."

Her fingers touched his hand where it was fisted on the armrest. "You're a good guy, Billy. It was me who screwed it

60

up."

His stomach twisted at her words. "God, do you really think that?"

"Of course." Her eyes were shiny. "It's what I do."

"It was just one night, Shannon," he said. "Just one night and back into the friend zone."

"Friend zone." She flicked her hair back from her face, an obviously restless gesture. "Oh, I hate that term."

That surprised him, and pissed him off a little bit. "You wanted to be friends. Should I have stopped hanging around?"

"No!" She covered her face with her hands now. "Billy, I just wanted… I don't know what I wanted."

"That's the thing, isn't it?"

She lowered her hands and looked at him, sweetly vulnerable and so tempting. "What's the thing?"

"I thought you wanted me," he said.

***

Shannon stared at Billy, seeing for the first time how she'd hurt him. She'd hurt herself too, hadn't she?

"Billy." She reached out for him, needing to touch him. Needing to wipe that hurt from his eyes. "I wanted you."

They stared at each other for a long minute, their breathing the only sound besides the hum of the big engine under the hood of his SUV.

"You wanted me."

It wasn't a question, but she nodded anyway. "I still do."

He sucked in a breath and pulled her closer. His lips were so soft against her throat. His hands fit so right on her body. His voice was rough and sweet in the quiet of his SUV. They were still parked in front of Rancho Casa, but the streetlight was out above them. It was dark. Close. And intimate.

Curling into him, Shannon breathed in his fresh scent. "Billy." She had nothing else. Just his name that came out in a soft moan.

His lips moved against her skin for a heart-stopping second before he pulled back. "Sorry."

She stared up at him, into his gorgeous eyes, and shook her head. "Don't apologize."

"We should go." He made no move to start the engine, though. "I should drive you back to Crescent and leave this alone."

Licking her lips, oh she wanted a taste of his sculpted lips, and nodded. "You should."

The light in his eyes dimmed a little. Letting out a breath, he moved to start the car.

She put her hand on his arm. "Wait."

He ran his gaze over her face, his lips parted. "Shannon."

"Kiss me, Billy."

He didn't hesitate. He brought those soft lips to hers and tasted her. Sparks struck her at first contact. As his tongue stroked hers, heat spread through her. It had been so long since she'd been kissed like this. Heck, she'd never been kissed like this since Billy. She had to get closer to him somehow. Just to see where this kiss could go.

"Shannon," he rasped, shifting her out of her seat until she was in his lap. "Damn, Shannon."

She pressed herself so close to him, her breasts aching as she rubbed against his hard chest. His big hands were on her butt, moving her to grind deliciously against him. Only fabric separated them and in the back of her mind she acknowledged that was a good thing despite her growing frustration.

They were in public, despite the darkness that shrouded them. But his windows were tinted, like just about any car's in Florida. She could indulge her curiosity for a few more minutes, couldn't she? Give in just a little bit to temptation?

"Make me feel good, Billy," she breathed, letting her head fall back. "Please."

He murmured something against her throat, using the tip of his tongue to stroke over her skin. "You drank your weight in Margaritas, Shannon."

She shrugged. "Maybe. But I also ate my weight in tamales."

He chuckled, the sound low and unbelievably hot. "True, but where you're concerned that's not a lot."

She touched his face, feeling the bristles of his cheeks on her palms as she drew him to her. "I'm not drunk, Billy."

He clasped his long fingers around her wrists, studying her before giving a quick shake of his head. "No. You're not."

"So kiss me."

"What about being friends?"

"You're just here for a couple of weeks, right?"

His lips thinned. "An expiration date? Is that what you

want?"

"What I want is to feel good. Do you remember what that's like, Billy?" She ran her hands over his broad shoulders, his strong arms. "Feeling good?"

He closed his eyes and cursed softly. "I remember everything about that night."

Her belly squeezed tight. That night. The night they'd made love.

"Me, too," she admitted on a whisper.

He worked his hands up under her gauzy blouse, his touch sending shivers through her. His mouth was on her breasts now, first through her bra and then with nothing to shield her from his mouth. His lips tugged on one nipple and she gasped.

"So beautiful," he said, giving her flesh a long lick. "So sweet."

He worked his clever fingers on the button of her pants and then his fingers were there. In her panties. Touching her just right.

"Yes." She spread her thighs as much as the seat allowed, letting out a low moan. "Right there."

Billy's mouth pulled hard on her nipple as his fingers

moved inside of her. Trembling, she clutched at his shoulders again. She was close. He must have guessed that, because he began to circle her clit with his thumb.

"Come, baby," he said, the brush of his breath making her damp nipple pucker. "Come for me."

In the next breath she did. Sobbing, she squeezed her eyes shut as she rode him to release. When she finally looked at him she saw his jaw was set. He was hard beneath her and she wanted to just throw the whole "friend" thing out the tinted windows. She wasn't ready for that, though. Not now. Maybe not ever. But she could make him feel as good as she did just now.

She unbuttoned his pants and unzipped them.

"Shannon," he said on a breath.

She pushed his boxer briefs down and freed him. He was huge and hot in her hands. "Let me make you feel good, Billy."

He swallowed audibly, his throat working. "You don't have to."

"I know." She brought her face to his as she stroked him. "I want to."

She kissed him as she drove him crazy, unable to keep

from tasting his lips again. Burying her face in the crook of his neck, she breathed him in as she brought him to orgasm with her hands.

His arms were tight around her as he began to shudder. Groaning long and low, he finally gave in to her. She leaned slightly away from him as he let his head fall back on the headrest.

She kissed his jaw once. "Good?" she teased.

He took in a deep breath and lifted his head, pinning her with those beautiful blue eyes. "You're magic, you know that?"

She stilled. No one had ever said that. "It was just fooling around. No big."

His mouth turned down a little before he shrugged. "Okay."

Maybe it was the afterglow of the first orgasm she'd had in months, but she suddenly felt chilly.

"Let's call it a night?" she asked him.

He tucked himself back into his pants and nodded. "Sure."

As they drove back to Crescent, she didn't say a word. She didn't look at him, either.

He gave her a soft kiss good night before she started her car, then pulled back. "Good night, Shannon."

She gave a shaky nod. "Good night."

As she drove away, she tried to get her head on straight. Feeling his hands on her, and getting her hands on him, was all very heady. And dangerous.

She'd always screwed everything up. Despite how good they'd both made each other feel, she couldn't help but think that she'd just screwed this up too.

Chapter 6

Thursday morning Billy woke in his luxurious guest room, all alone. He'd gone over everything and that had happened between him and Shannon last night, still amazed that they'd managed to give each other a little something-something in the front seat of his new SUV. It had been mutual masturbation, true. But hotter than any action he'd had in the months since they were together.

He hadn't been lying when he'd told her she was magic, though. She was everything, and if he'd thought he was over her he sure as hell realized now that he wasn't.

"Shit." He grumbled a few more choice words as he climbed out of bed.

He grabbed his swim trunks and went into the huge bathroom to start his day. He had nothing to do until tomorrow's meeting with Jo out at her goat farm, and he wasn't in any mood to get shot down by Shannon. Not after what they'd shared last night. It might have changed the way he saw his life going forward, but for her? It was just fooling around.

"Like hell it was," he said as he left the room.

It was early, not quite eight o'clock, but he could see

that there were already several people on the beach. They could have it today. He wanted to swim and swim hard, and the pool was empty right now. That shouldn't be a surprise. If he was on vacation he'd spend a lot of his time taking in the view of the bay and sitting on that sugar-soft sand. He wasn't on vacation, though. He'd never really been, had he?

Back when his parents were alive, the three of them would sometimes head out to the Orlando theme parks for day trips. Or they'd drive east to the coast over in Melbourne. They'd both worked too hard and too long to give up more than an odd day here and there to spend as a family. His mother had been a waitress in a diner and his father had been an assistant manager of the big box store in town. That night their car crashed, during a summer storm when he'd been ten years old, had ended any hope of their lives getting any easier. It sure hadn't for him. He still missed them every day.

He found the stack of thick, plush towels meant for guests' use and grabbed one, tossing it onto the nearest lounge chair. After a quick rinse under the outdoor shower, he dove into the pool and started swimming. Back and forth. Back and forth. Again and again, until his blood pounded in his ears and his muscles screamed.

Gripping onto the edge of the pool, he finally stopped and sucked in a great breath. Rolling under again, he began to cool down as he slowed his pace up and down the length of the pool a few more times.

Surfacing, he slicked his hair back off of his face and pulled himself out of the pool. He padded over to where he'd left his towel. Rubbing it over his face and chest, he breathed in deeply through his nose and exhaled with a grunt. His heartbeat was slowing to normal as he ran the towel over his hair.

"Looking good, Billy Goat."

He lowered the towel to find Carrie from the spa shop grinning at him. "Good morning to you, too."

She opened her mouth like she was about to say something, and then bit her lip. She smiled over his shoulder toward something or someone, and he turned his head to see what had caught her attention. Shannon stood there, dressed for work and obviously just coming in. Her lips parted as she ran her gaze all over his dripping body. Christ, with the way she was staring at him he was close to tenting his trunks.

"Hey, Shannon," he managed to say.

Her eyes slowly made their way back up to his face and

she blinked. "Billy." Her voice was breathy and sent a shiver through him that had nothing to do with the perfectly-cooled pool water dripping down his back.

Carrie giggled as she passed him. "See you inside, Shannon."

Shannon said something to her friend but Billy was too caught by her gaze to actually make it out. He stepped closer to her, seeing the heat in her eyes that wasn't exactly something you'd have for a friend. Was she thinking about having her hands all over him last night? About having his hands, his lips, on her body?

"Work," she said.

He tilted his head, keeping his smile to himself as she obviously enjoyed the view. It made a guy feel good, to have a girl look at him like that. Especially if that particular girl was the one he wanted to get closer to and soon.

"Work, huh?" he asked, his lips twitching.

She seemed to collect herself as she nodded, holding her purse close to her middle. "Yeah. Yes. I have to get to work."

He spread his arms wide. "Don't let me keep you."

She did that body-scan thing with her eyes again, and then hurried past him. As she neared the doors to the lobby she stared at him again over her shoulder. Now he grinned. He couldn't help it.

Damn, it felt good to see that she wanted him. Even if she denied it, it was clear on her face. That look was pure hunger, and if he didn't get himself back in the pool anybody who walked through here would see his reaction to Shannon's gaze on his body.

Dropping the towel back on the lounge chair, he lowered himself into the pool to chill his dick a little. He just floated, keeping his lower half beneath the surface until he brought himself back in control. That look from her was very interesting. They were just fooling around last night, she'd said. No big, she'd said.

She could say whatever she liked. He knew this wasn't just a game. This wasn't fooling around. She might not realize it, but he was playing for keeps.

***

Shannon's heart was still racing as she all but ran into the spa to hide behind her desk. Oh, the sight of Billy still wet from the pool made her think all kinds of things. Naughty things. Dangerous things. Things she had no right to think about with her so-called friend.

73

"That was a nice way to start a day," Carrie said with a laugh as she went into the spa shop.

Shannon gave her a noncommittal shrug, powering up her computer in order to have something to do with her hands. They were still tingling from just being near Billy. Had he looked like that the night they'd been together? Her apartment had been dark, she remembered. He'd felt incredible to her touch, and the sounds and scents of that night were tattooed on her memory. But seeing him like that this morning? Carrie was right. It was a great way to start her day.

His long, strong legs had been braced apart. His arms working as he ran the towel over his hair. He was tanned, which she guessed was from working outdoors. He'd always seemed like a capable kind of guy. And oh, that chest. Broad and sculpted, and dusted with just the right amount of dark hair. That dark hair thinned to a line that led her gaze over his ridged abs to a sliver of lighter skin revealed by the low-slung waistband of his swim trunks.

She'd been dumbstruck. There was no other word for it. And Billy, that tease, had enjoyed her discomfort. Those blue eyes of his had danced and his mouth had curved into a smile she'd wanted to kiss off of his face.

"How was dinner last night?" Marion asked.

Shannon took in a breath before facing her boss. "It was good. We went to Rancho Casa."

"I heard."

Shannon's heart gave a thump. "What, exactly, did you hear?"

Marion gave her a sly smile, running her hand over the counter as she made a show of thinking about her answer. Shannon refrained from shouting at her to just spit it out, seeing as the woman was her boss and all.

"You and your friend the goat guy, who also took you to lunch yesterday by the way, were all over each other."

"What?"

"Billing and cooing over *tamales* and margaritas?"

Shannon's face felt like it was on fire. Her boss had to see her blush. She shared her sister's light coloring, and she guessed her cheeks were really pink right now.

"Billing and cooing? Not really. Just old friends catching up." Shannon gave her a weak smile. "Dinner was fantastic."

Marion nodded. "Will and I have to get there and soon.

I'm starting to go into withdrawal for their *chimichangas*. Maybe we'll get a babysitter for tomorrow night."

"Sure."

Shannon was only half-listening at this point. She was just so relieved that Marion hadn't been talking about her front-seat fooling-around with Billy after dinner.

"I'll let you get to it," Marion said. "Another busy one today."

Shannon said something in agreement, holding her breath until her boss went back into her office. Once she checked on the appointments scheduled for today, she closed her eyes and gave in to the temptation of picturing Billy as he'd looked out by the pool. Yum. She'd seen her share of hot guys, and been with more than her share, but none of them compared to him. Considering he was also a nice guy? He was so not for her. She'd turn him into a jerk somehow. It was her secret power.

Lunch time rolled around, and Marion gave everyone an hour to get out of the spa and reenergize. She planned to eat at her desk though, without the distraction of Billy just across the table. She ducked out to the coffee shop in the lobby to grab a salad and a yogurt.

As the kid behind the counter rang her up, she realized she'd been eating much more healthy since she'd been in Serenity Shores. It must be a side effect of working at an organic spa. The setting and environment was both energizing and relaxing, as surprising as that was. It felt really good, starting this life far from her old one. There was Billy, though. He was a big part of her past, even if he didn't know it.

Taking her healthy lunch in hand, she settled at one of the small tables dotting the coffee shop and cracked open her bottle of sparkling water.

"I've got his room number, you know."

Shannon looked at Carrie as she joined her. "Whose room number?"

"Right." Carrie smirked as she tore the top off of her yogurt. "Billy Goat, Shannon. He's in room two-thirty-eight. God, he's hot. Tell me you don't want to hit that?"

Memories of last night popped into her head but she shoved them away. If she blushed in front of Carrie, the girl would know just how much she'd hit that. And just how much she wanted to hit that even more. Maybe in room 238.

"He's good looking," Shannon said.

"Yeah, he's good looking." Carrie snorted. "And Crescent is just a nice place to stay."

Shannon laughed. "All right. He's hotter than the sun. Is that what you me to say?"

"It's a start," Carrie said with a wink.

Shannon sipped her sparkling water, thinking about how amazing Billy had looked this morning. "Okay, he's the hottest guy I've ever seen. And when I saw him this morning, dripping wet from the pool, I wanted to peel those swim trunks off of him and lick him dry."

Apparently there was no shocking Carrie, because the girl just let out a shout of laughter. Suddenly she stilled. "Shannon…"

Shannon held up a hand. "I've told you just how much I want the guy, Carrie. Isn't that enough?"

"It is for me," Billy said from behind her.

Shannon closed her eyes, saying a silent prayer that he hadn't heard everything she'd said. She could feel him behind her. Could smell him, that fresh scent she believed she'd always associate with him.

Turning slightly in her chair, she craned her neck to face him. He wore tan cargo shorts again, with a frosty blue vintage-looking T-shirt. Both garments fit him just right.

"Hi, Billy," she said.

His eyes were sparkling like they had beside the pool. "Hi, Shannon."

"Join us!" Carrie said, dragging a chair over from the nearest table.

He arched one brow and Shannon shrugged in answer to his unspoken question. Folding his tall frame, he sat very close to Shannon and took the lid off of his coffee drink.

"How are you ladies today?" he asked.

"Fine," Carrie said, her eyes running over Billy. "Just fine."

Shannon tried to glare at her but the girl couldn't be cowed, either.

Carrie jumped up, gathering her things as she did so. "I forgot I have to make a call," she chirped. "Catch you later, Shannon."

Shannon watched her go and waited for Billy to ease away from her. He didn't, and she wasn't really surprised. His leg was pressed against hers under the table and his bared forearms looked very strong resting there on the table.

"Did you have a good swim this morning?" she asked,

eager to fill the silence.

"Yep." He stared at her for a second. "Did you have a good look?"

Heat flashed over her as she recalled just how good a look she'd gotten. She rolled her eyes instead of letting him know how she hadn't been able to forgot that look.

"Okay, you're hot," she said. "This is news?"

He shrugged a shoulder and leaned closer. "A guy likes to know when a girl wants to, how did you put it?" he asked in a low voice. "Lick me until I'm dry?"

Now her face was on fire. "Please," she whispered.

"Name the time and place," he said.

It was her turn to laugh. She felt a bubble grow inside her chest. How could wanting and liking both be swirling in her head? She definitely more than wanted him. Did she more than like him, too? Yes. This was Billy, after all. Sweet, hot as F, Billy.

"Seven o'clock tonight," she whispered. "Room two-thirty-eight."

His well-formed mouth dropped open. "My room." He sucked in a breath. "You're serious."

"I am." She reached over and covered his hand with

hers like she had last night. "You're only here for a little while, right?"

"Until next Friday, yeah," he said.

She let him see how much she wanted to spend some naughty time with him. He was the rare combination: a good time and a good guy.

"Then why not?" she asked.

His brow furrowed a little before he gave her a wide smile. "That's not the question, Shannon."

His voice sounded rough and she felt it like a caress.

"No?" she asked.

"No," he said. "The question is, how the hell am I going to wait until tonight?"

She moved her hand up his arm to his bicep. "Hashtag guy problems."

Chapter 7

Billy looked through the room-service menu for the fifteenth time. There was no way he was going to waste time going out to dinner with Shannon tonight. He felt that expiration date looming, and it wasn't just next Friday. He was afraid that at any second she'd decide he wasn't worth her time. Hadn't she set him aside before?

"Don't borrow trouble, dumb ass," he grumbled to himself.

She was coming to his room tonight, and he'd make sure to give her a night she would want to repeat this time. Over and over again, if things went his way.

He called down to order a couple of steaks, and a salmon dinner too in case the burger she ate the other day was a once-in-a-while thing, and a couple of desserts. Delivery time was set for seven-thirty. He didn't want it to look like he was rushing her. That was for damn sure. And the time before dinner would be spent talking, and maybe messing around.

In the months between their first night together and that night he'd fucked it up, they'd been able to talk. Really talk. He missed that almost as much as he had kissing her. Loving her.

He had about a half hour to kill, so he went over his list of questions for Jo Potter tomorrow. She had an Animal Science degree like he did, and she was running an operation he'd love to emulate. She was also planning for something that could be wildly successful, and he wanted to know just how to get his own dream up and running.

He would ask her opinion on the best breed he should raise, and how she ran her own breeding program. Her expertise was legendary, and that wasn't even taking into consideration her soap-making which she had risen to an art form. He glanced over at the stack of bars he'd bought at the spa shop and wondered which one would be Shannon's favorite. He was getting her into that big tub for sure. Maybe not tonight, but it would be a way to entice her to come back to his room another time before he went back to St. Cloud.

That thought soured his mood a little. He knew he was leaving in about a week. She knew it too, and it seemed to be the only reason she was giving in to the heat between them. It was there. For sure. The way she'd looked at him this morning? Damn. Even she couldn't deny it any longer.

He sat on the sleek couch in the sitting area, opened his tablet, and scrolled through the saved web pages in his browser. There seemed to be tons of sites dedicated to helping someone start up a goat farm. What breeds give the best-tasting milk and the best milk for soap-making. What to feed the little guys. How often to breed them. What milk production could be expected. Whether to have a male goat, or buck, on hand or to farm out the breeding.

He'd heard about Hamilton, Jo's buck. The goat was rumored to be a son-of-a-bitch and, since Billy wanted the petting zoo to be kid friendly, maybe he would stick to does and doelings. And maybe a castrated wether or two if his does gave birth to any males. Wethers were supposed to be pretty docile.

He clicked through pictures of the Nigerian Dwarf goats. They were pretty cute. The Nubians were a little bit taller, which might make milking easier for him. The goats he'd seen in St. Cloud were Nubians, which were also pretty good looking and friendly animals. Maybe he'd ask Shannon her opinion, too. If she had input on what he was planning, maybe she'd come visit some time.

"Fuck that," he said, putting his tablet back to sleep.

She didn't want to visit Cypress any more than she wanted to go back to St. Cloud. He wished he could blame the string of assholes she'd dated, but she was a big girl. She'd made her choices, even if he never knew just what she was thinking as she'd made them. He wasn't such a catch six months ago either, though. True, he'd never mistreated her. He'd cut off his left nut before he'd ever consciously hurt her. But he hadn't fought for her, either. Nope. He'd let her shove him into the fucking friend zone. After tonight, he hoped he never see the place again.

Right before seven o'clock, there was a knock at his door. His belly clenched and he fisted his hands. Christ, you'd think he'd never had a date before. He crossed to the door and opened it to find Shannon standing there. She looked as hot as she had the night before, wearing another soft-looking embroidered shirt but trading her pants for a skirt that came to just above her knees. He tried not to stare, but for a little thing she had some kickass curves.

"Hey," he said, focusing on her beautiful face.

She smiled, tilting her head so her hair fell to one side. "Hey."

It was a move like the bartender had tried on him, but on Shannon? It sent a rush of want through him. He reached out to gently tugged her into the room, unable to keep from kissing her. Her lips clung to his for a second, and then he pressed his brow to hers.

"I ordered room service," he told her.

She laughed softly, bringing her hand up to his face. "In a hurry, Billy Goat?"

He slowly shook his head. "I don't want to waste any time tonight. Do you?"

She bit her lip, her eyes wide. "Nope."

He shut the door behind her and watched as she walked around the guest room.

"This is amazing," she said, her fingers trailing over the modern furniture until she reached the glass doors leading to the balcony. "Whoa."

He joined her, sliding the doors open to the view. The sun was low but sunset was an hour or so away. The Gulf was calm, the waves lapping against the sand two stories down. The balcony was private, and big enough for an upholstered lounge and a small table with two chairs.

She stepped out onto the balcony, gripping the railing as she tipped her head back. "Oh, this view."

He agreed, thinking he could stare at her all night. The low orange sun kissed her face and lit her hair. The breeze kicked up, pinning her shirt to her front and outlining every curve he'd dreamed about all last night.

He studied the sleek muscles of her legs as she flexed and shifted on her sandaled feet. Coming up behind her, he clasped her shoulders. She shifted, turning her face up to his with a smile.

"I like your room, Billy."

He ran his hands down her arms to clasp hers. "I like you in my room, Shannon."

He kissed her again, feeling that rush of heat that was never far when she was near. Their tongues tangled and he wrapped his arms around her. With one hand splayed on her back and the other cupping half of her ass, he pressed against her and let her know just how she was affecting him.

When she made a soft purring sound, he urged her down on that chaise lounge and worked his hands up under her skirt. Her skin was smooth as silk, and hot under his fingers. Glancing up at her, he saw that she was watching him from beneath her lashes.

"I want to make you happy, Shannon," he said, kissing the inside of her left knee. He stared into her eyes, fighting to keep his words light and teasing. "Let me make you happy?"

***

Shannon was spread-eagle on the marshmallow-soft chaise lounge, with Billy's big hands running over her inner thighs. He had callouses that rubbed her skin just the right way, and her pulse was racing as he kissed her so close to her center.

There was something in his eyes, their blue darker and more intense, as he asked for something they both obviously wanted. She'd felt him, hard and huge against her belly there at the railing. She felt the trembling in his fingers as he teased her through her lace panties now.

Biting her lip again, she nodded. "Please, Billy."

He flashed that Billy smile for a split-second before he stripped off her panties and licked her. Sparks lit from that delicious point of contact, and she gripped the sides of the chaise lounge as he drove her crazy. He was humming now, obviously enjoying himself as he slowly loved her with his mouth. His tongue and teeth joined in the fun as he stroked his hands over her fevered flesh. She'd never been so turned on so quickly. She was close. When two of his big fingers began to move inside of her, she lost any grip on her composure she'd had.

Sucking in a breath, she trembled as pleasure spiraled up inside her as glorious as the sunset. He was relentless, licking and nibbling as she came again and again. When she came back to herself, she found his face in front of hers. His eyes were dancing now, and she couldn't resist kissing his lips.

"That was amazing," she murmured.

"I love making you come," he growled. "Damn, you're sweet."

He was the sweet one. He always was. She wouldn't read into his words, though. He had to be feeling pretty good right now, since she couldn't remember when she'd ever lost herself so completely. It was all his doing.

He eased her legs back together and as he sat beside her she saw he held himself awkwardly. The reason was clear as she ran her eyes over him. The front of his very nice linen trousers was tented. He was in a bad way and she knew what she could do. She could give him a little bit of what he'd just given her.

Cupping him, she gave him a stroke. He leaned back on his hands, his throat working.

"Shannon." Her name was a plea on his lips. "Please."

"Oh, yes." She unbuttoned his shirt first. She had to see that magnificent chest again, and she stroked his heated skin with her hands flat on his pecs. "Mmm, Billy."

She reached inside his pants and freed him as she had last night, but this time she sank to knees and took him in her mouth. He groaned as she worked him.

"Your mouth." His hand cupped her head gently. "God."

She ran her fingers over him as she licked him, teasing and taunting him until he was very close. He groaned again, his hips moving as she sucked him deep into her mouth. It didn't take long before she pushed him over the edge, making him buck as he surrendered.

Smiling up at him, she rested her hands on one of his strong thighs. "Good?"

"Good?" He cursed softly. "Shannon, I can't even think of a word that could do that justice."

He gently grasped her arms and drew her up to him. Turning, he fell back on the chaise and she happily draped herself over him. His chest was bare as his shirt fell completely open, and she dropped kissed on his skin. He smelled so good. Fresh and creamy.

"Is that soap from the spa shop I smell?" she asked.

He ran his fingers through her hair, his chest moving as he chuckled softly. "I told you I was going to do research."

Wriggling against him, she brought her face to his again. "Maybe later we can try it out in that bathtub with a view you told me about."

His eyes darkened again and he began to kiss her. A sharp rapping came at the door and he pulled back. "Shit. Dinner."

"Then let's eat, Billy." She leaned away from him and patted his chest, unable to keep from stroking his skin before lifting her hand away from him. "We have all night."

"All night?" He stood, his brows were raised. "You sure?"

"If we just have tonight, why not spend it together?"

His mouth tightened a little as he buttoned his shirt and tucked it into his trousers. "Why just tonight exactly?"

She looked away from him as she straightened her own clothes. "I'm not very good at more than 'just tonight,' Billy."

"We'll have to see about that." That brought her gaze back to him. He dropped a wink. "Your panties are under the lounger."

Her cheeks heated as he strolled back into the room to answer the door. Billy's deep rumbling voice mingled with the room-service waiter's deferential one. She wasn't going back in there until she was more composed. Or at least dressed. After that "just tonight" discussion her thoughts were a little bit jumbled. Although that could be due to the mind-blowing orgasms he'd just given her.

She stared out at the spectacular view again, trying to rein in her emotions. Billy had been a good friend for some time now. A fantastic lover that one night, and it seemed like he'd only gotten better in that department. He was dangerous, though. A good guy who couldn't possibly stay that way once she worked her particular brand of mojo on him. Her bad choices were legendary, and she hated to even think of painting him with that same brush.

Speaking of paint, the sun was very low now and the water appeared splashed with reds and pinks and oranges. If they just had one night, and she wasn't as sure about that as she thought she should be, this was a pretty perfect start for it.

"Come on, baby," Billy said from inside. "Dinner's served."

Straightening her spine, she went back into his

ridiculously-amazing guest room and found their meal set beautifully on the small table in the sitting area. China and crystal elevated the settings, and the dishes looked like they'd just been served at a five-star restaurant and not brought up to a guest's room.

But more tempting than anything on that pristine white tablecloth was the man himself. She would have to keep her heart out of this. It was known for its stupidity and for choosing the wrong guy time after time. She'd keep things light with Billy and wouldn't worry about how she would feel when he went back home next week.

She wouldn't fall hard and fast. She wouldn't be the old Shannon. No. She would be the new-and-improved Shannon even if it meant making sure that Billy went back to St. Cloud and forgot all about her.

Chapter 8

Billy snuggled close to Shannon on the couch. They'd shared their amazing dinner, damn those steaks were good, and now each ate from their own plate of the chef's dessert special, strawberry shortcake.

"This reminds me of something from the little bakery in Cypress," she said.

"Yeah?" he asked. "I stopped by the coffee shop a couple of times, but I didn't see a bakery."

"It's phenomenal." She licked the whipped cream off of her fork with a soft moan. "There's an ice cream shop, too."

"Sounds like you got to know the place pretty well." He used his thumb to wipe a drop of whipped cream from her lip, which she licked off of him. Man, that tongue of hers. "I didn't know you were there all that long."

She stilled for a second and then shrugged. "I moved there after Rob-the-dick and I imploded."

He wanted to ask her why she'd gotten together with the guy in the first place, but knew it wasn't any of his business. She didn't know Billy pined after her for months. After what they'd shared out on the balcony before dinner, and what he hoped they would share later in that big bed, the last thing he wanted to do was play the jealous lover.

"So what, about two months?" he asked.

"Give or take."

He took her plate and put it with his on the leather ottoman in front of the couch. "Did you like it there?"

She chuckled in answer and he looked back at her.

"What?" he asked.

"Stepford, Billy. That's what you called Cypress."

He dipped his head, giving her a smile. "Yeah well, I guess I was stuck in that mindset. I used to be a St. Cloud townie, remember?"

"Used to be?"

"Hey, now," he laughed a little. "I'm taking the money my uncle left me and moving there to start my farm. I won't be a townie anymore."

She blinked. "You're going to live there?"

"I hope to. Goats don't need a lot of work, but you do have to milk them twice a day. Taking care of the critters, running a petting zoo…it would make sense to live out there."

Her brow crinkled at that, so he grabbed his tablet and brought up some pictures of the goats.

"Here. Look at these little guys," he said. "Wouldn't

you want to live near them?"

Shannon tucked her legs beneath her and leaned closer to him as she peered at the photos.

"Oh, they're adorable!" she said, pointing to one of the Nubians. "Look at that long face, Billy. They look so serious. It cracks me up."

"I think those are the kind I'm going to get for the farm. They're Nubians, and a little bit taller than these girls." He flicked over to another photo. "These are Nigerian Dwarves."

"So cute. How do you know about this stuff? Did your uncle have goats?"

"Nope. Cattle and horses, but no goats."

"Then how?"

"I was a vet tech when I was a kid, and then I got my Animal Science degree from UF. I learned about different breeding practices, stuff like that."

"That's very cool." She looked at the tablet again, delight on her face, and then placed her hand on his leg. "These little guys are adorable. How can you pick? Can you get both?"

"Tell you what." He set the tablet back on the ottoman next to their empty plates. "When it comes time to pick them out, you can come with me."

"Where?"

"St. Cloud. There are a few farms I've been to that have stock."

She shook her head. "Thanks, but I'm not going back to St. Cloud. Not ever."

"It would be that hard to run into Rob-the-dick?" he asked, trying to keep his tone light.

"It's not just him. I was never very careful about how people saw me. I just didn't think that far ahead."

"And now?"

"Now I care about my reputation. People like me here."

"People liked you there," he pointed out.

She blew out a breath. "Guys liked me, Billy."

The expression on her face was so sad he couldn't keep himself from taking her hands as he had on the balcony.

"Shannon, don't be so down on yourself. You're a wonderful person."

Her eyes were shiny as she stared up at him. "Why do you say that? I was a so-so employee at best. A lousy girlfriend. And a crappy sister."

"You love your sister, right?"

"Yes." She didn't hesitate. "We were just starting to reconnect, actually."

"When you came down here?"

She nodded.

"You came to a brand new place, impressed your boss enough to get a job you're obviously great at, and seem like you fit in."

"So? Lots of people do that."

"Not me."

"What do you mean?"

He couldn't talk about how much like an outsider he'd always felt. The orphan. The suck-up. The misfit. Even his uncle, who it turned out really had cared for him, had treated him with as much affection as one of his horses.

"I don't want to talk about the past, Shannon. Do you?"

He knew she'd put the past in her rearview when she'd come to Serenity Shores. He was in that mirror too, though. At least he had been, until he'd walked into Crescent and run smack into the girl he couldn't forget.

"I couldn't get you out of my mind after that night six months ago," he said, tugging her closer. "Now that you're in my arms tonight, I'm not going to let you go."

***

Shannon's breath caught at the affection she saw in Billy's eyes. What was he talking about, not letting her go? Tonight? She couldn't believe he meant anything more than that, except maybe the rest of his visit here at the most. Having Billy love her, though? Getting as close as she could to this man? That was so very tempting.

"You want me in your arms, Billy Goat?" she teased.

He barked out a laugh and grabbed her, standing up to hold her tight against his chest. "That's enough about goats tonight, Shannon."

She held on to his shoulders as he carried her over to the bed. Dropping her, he followed her down and covered her with his big body. The heat between them, sometimes banked but never doused, flared to life. Almost before she was aware, he had her stripped. Completely this time, and the expression on his face told her he liked what he saw.

"You're beautiful, do you know that?" he asked, his voice low.

She leaned up on her elbows, bringing a hand to the open collar of his shirt. "You're so good for my ego."

His eyes raked her again, making her tingle. "Happy to

help, but it's not my fault if you can't see how fucking gorgeous you are."

She'd heard a lot of lines from a lot of guys. Customers at the End Zone, hook-ups and short-lived boyfriends had complimented her. She was cute. She was hot. She was pretty. Words like beautiful and gorgeous? Never. And coming from Billy, the compliments felt sincere. That was the sexiest thing she could imagine.

"Strip, Billy," she said. "I want to see all of you, too."

He did as she asked, and quicker than she could have hoped for. Like she'd seen this morning at the pool, his body was masculine perfection. Tall and broad, and sculpted from his pecs to his abs. He had those two sexy dents on either side of his butt, and as he came back to the bed she saw that wasn't too shabby either.

"You're beautiful, Billy," she whispered.

He shook his head, brushing his hair back from his brow. "Flattery will get you everything."

Her nipples tightened as he cupped one of her breasts. "Good," she sighed. "I want everything."

His eyes flared and he kissed her. Oh, he was such a good kisser. As he had earlier on the balcony, he moved his hands and touched her in all the right places. In all the right ways. His tongue was skilled as it burned a trail down her neck. His fingers teased her between her thighs, and she opened wider to his touch.

He kissed her again, cupping her face as he stared down at her. "Is this really happening?" His breath came fast and she caught his urgency. "Or am I having a wet dream?"

She reached down to grasp him and he shivered. "Real enough for you?"

He growled at her and then grinned. "Oh, yeah."

He reached one hand over the side of the bed and fished a condom out of his pants pocket. "This is going to be fast, Shannon." He kissed her again, hungrily, like he couldn't get enough of her. "Hard and fast."

His words sent another wave of intense want through her. "Good."

A few more seconds of kisses and caresses and he was there. She flashed back to their last night together, and she recalled just how perfect he'd fit then. It was the same tonight, but better somehow. She was different. Heck, he was different. Still sweet and hot, but with a determination to give them both what they needed. It was nearly overwhelming and she squeezed her eyes shut.

Every stroke was perfect, every move just what she needed. Digging her heels into the plush bed, she arched as her first climax hit. Flushing hot and cold, she grabbed on to his biceps as he continued to move just right above her.

"So good, baby," he rasped, bringing his face to the side of her neck. The scruff on his jaw felt rough and hot. "So damn good."

She cried out, losing herself again. She heard him shout his own release as if from far away. Holding him close, she stroked her fingers through his hair as he dropped kisses on her heated skin.

The balcony doors were still open, and now that they were quiet she could hear the waves against the sand. The room was lit by a fiery sunset and if she could rouse the energy she'd go out there and see it up close.

After what felt like seconds or hours, she wasn't exactly sure which, she opened her eyes to find him gazing down at he again. He wore an adorably dopey smile and a look of intense satisfaction on his handsome face.

"You're incredible, do you know that?" he asked.

"That was all you," she said with a sigh.

"Yeah? Then you should stay tonight. I'll let you make it up to me."

For a second, she wanted to. Wanted to spend the whole night with him in this amazing bed. She couldn't. She knew what could happen with that kind of attachment.

"I have work in the morning." It was the truth, but it felt like a lame excuse.

"Yeah." He fell to her side and held her close. "And I have my meeting out at Jo Potter's."

"Then I should go."

She made a move to sit up but he grabbed her hips and pulled her back down beneath him.

"I'll let you go in a little while, I promise," he said.

Her stomach flipped. "And just what will we do in that little while, Billy?"

The smile he gave her made the bed tip beneath her. Oh, this was dangerous. But for tonight, she'd push her worries aside and let Billy love her again.

Chapter 9

Billy drove back from Jo Potter's place, his mind full of ideas. She'd been so welcoming, and full of information. Her husband, millionaire Ethan Potter, had crossed his arms and glared at Billy like he thought he had designs on the pretty brunette. That attitude was short-lived, though. It had to be clear to anybody with eyes that Jo was head over heels in love with her husband. When Billy and Jo began to talk goats and milk and soaps, the guy obviously realized he was on the up and up.

As he'd talked with them, he'd learned that he and Ethan actually had a lot in common. He'd fallen ass-backwards into money due to a small real estate investment that had paid off in spades, and Billy felt like his money had also come through no effort on his part. True, it took a lot longer for Ethan to count his money. Billy was small potatoes in that department. His inheritance was more than enough to build his dream, though.

His dream. Last night with Shannon had exceeded everything he'd fantasized about since their first time. On the balcony. In his bed. Even talking on the couch had felt so real. When he'd gotten her to stay as late as she'd dared to, he'd loved her two more times before finally letting her drive home.

The farm wasn't far from Crescent, and soon he was pulling in to park at the resort. He wanted to talk to Shannon, and tell her everything he planned for his own place. Jo Potter had given him lots to think about, and he couldn't wait to get Shannon's take on it. She might not know it yet, but she was part of his plans. He wasn't buying a ring or anything, but when he pictured his house and farm? She was there with him.

"Don't count on that, Billy boy," he told himself.

Shannon was dead-set against going back to St. Cloud, but she had to like Cypress Corners. Who the hell didn't like it? She couldn't get over her past. It didn't matter to him, but she was tender-hearted. It was one of the things he loved about her.

He turned off the ignition and sat, stunned. He loved her. He wanted to look out for her and make her smile. He wanted to do her every way to Sunday, and give her so much pleasure she couldn't do without him. He didn't give a shit about her past, but he had no idea how to prove that to her.

Stepping out into the afternoon heat, he grabbed his new

baseball cap from the seat. It was emblazoned with the name of the Serenity Shores Sand Dollars, the soccer club Ethan Potter was starting.

Billy walked into the lobby and was struck again by the gorgeous setting. The luxurious atmosphere extended to his guest room, and adding Shannon to the mix last night had brought it up to goddamn phenomenal.

Heading directly to the spa, he saw through the glass doors that she was seated behind her desk as he'd expected. She looked so sweet sitting there, her brow furrowed a little as she studied her computer screen. Her hair was shiny and her face bright, and he flattered himself to think that the loving he'd given her last night led to her blush of health today.

The doors slid open and she looked up. The next instant she smiled at him, and his gut twisted. His epiphany in the parking lot was fresh, after all. And the light in her big amber eyes told him she at least liked him a lot. It was a start.

"Hey, Shannon."

"How did your meeting go?"

Her interest gave him another point in his favor, he reasoned. "Great." He put on the baseball cap, turning it slightly to show her the front. "I'm a big fan."

Her brows arched. "The team doesn't exist yet."

He chuckled. "I'm a fan of the Potter's, of the farm and their plans for the complex, Shannon. I can't wait to replicate it, on a smaller scale of course, on my own property."

She crossed her arms and leaned back in her chair. "You're pretty psyched, aren't you?"

He grinned. "Beyond. When are you done here?"

She glanced at the screen. "In about forty-five minutes."

"Dinner then. With me."

"Okay. You want Mexican again?"

"Nope. I'll get us reservations at Wisteria."

"Seriously?"

He shrugged. "I'll sure give it a try."

"Let me make a call for you," a tall, dark-haired woman said as she came out of the back of the spa. "Hi, there. I'm Marion Tucker."

Billy shook her outstretched hand. "Billy Harris."

Shannon shared a smile with the woman and Billy saw once more that confidence he'd spied the first day. Shannon was coming into her own, and he wished he knew how to convince her that she could have that success back in

107

Cypress. With him.

"I can't ask you to make that call," he told her.

Marion waved a hand. "It's no trouble, Billy. The chef owes me a favor."

"Thanks, then."

"Hey, you're taking Shannon to Wisteria," she said. "I haven't been able to get her there in all the time she's worked here."

Shannon blushed, and she looked adorable. It was all he could do to stand there and not vault over the desk and kiss her crazy.

"So what time?" Marion asked.

"Is six thirty okay?" he asked Shannon.

"Sounds good." She glanced down at her uniform. "That will give me time to go home and change. Jeez, what am I going to wear?"

Marion clicked her tongue. "It's fancy food and atmosphere, Shannon. Not so much fancy in the dress code, since it's nestled in Crescent."

"I'll see you back here around six, Shannon." Billy lifted his chin in Marion's direction. "Thanks again. You're saving me."

"Hey, you're taking one of my best girls out for a fantastic meal. Win-win in my book."

Billy liked this woman. She obviously saw Shannon as the awesome girl he knew she was, and that was win-win in his book, too. Now if only Shannon could see herself that way.

***

Shannon lowered herself into the water, moving into Billy's arms. The scent and lather of the almond goat's-milk soap surrounded them. The tub in his guest room was beyond incredible, but the much-talked-about view was even more amazing.

He held her close, kissing her. His hands began to roam, and she marveled that she could want him again so soon after he'd loved her in his bed. Turning her, she snuggled between his bent legs, feeling evidence that he was getting happy again right behind her butt. His arms encircled her now.

"Damn, this is nice," he said, resting his chin on her shoulder.

She nodded, placing her hands on his forearms. Candles were lit on the wide window ledge, and the ambient lighting near the high ceilings set such a romantic mood she could

swoon right there and drown in the bathtub. The candles'
clean, fresh scent reminded her of Billy.

"Where did you get these candles?" she asked.

"Spa shop." He chuckled. "And didn't your friend
Carrie tease me about them."

"Yeah, once she found out you were taking me to
Wisteria she was all smug."

"Smug? About what?"

She glanced over her shoulder at him. "Don't look so
innocent. You overheard our conversation in the coffee
shop."

He flashed that Billy-smile. "You mean when you
admitted that you want me?"

She pinched his bicep. "I think we're way past that little
disclosure, don't you?"

"Mmm-hmm."

He nuzzled the side of her neck, sending tingles through
her. Had any other guy made her feel so much? She didn't
think so.

"I could stay here all night," she admitted.

His arms tensed for a second, and then he dropped
kisses on her skin. "You're more than welcome to. We'll send

down for food. I'll have to get more condoms, though."

She laughed. "Oh, yeah?"

He moved his hands up and down her arms, coming very close to her breasts. "To get through the weekend? Damn right. Wait. You're off for the weekend, aren't you?"

"I am. Saturdays are usually crammed full of events at the resort, weddings and things, so the days leading up to the weekend are always busy at the spa. Marion has another girl come in to run the desk on Saturday mornings."

"I like that woman," he said, his lips close to her ear. "She cares about you."

Shannon's belly did that twist thing. "She cares about everyone, Billy. I'm not special."

He tensed again, and then grabbed her shoulders to turn her in the water. "Listen to me." He stared at her hard, his mouth a thin line. "You're special. To your boss, sure. And to your sister, of course. But especially to me."

His look of utter sincerity made her feel like his compliments had last night. Wanted. Cherished. Like she mattered. Oh, how she wished she could believe him.

"Billy," she breathed.

He lost his serious expression, his sculpted lips curving

at the corners. "I'm thinking about doing something special to you right now, actually." He rubbed those big hands over her back down to her butt, holding her close to his erection. "What do you say?"

She put aside her wishes and wrapped her arms around his neck. "I say we make some bubbles."

He barked out a laugh and they did just that.

By Sunday afternoon, she thought she could easily get used to being around Billy. She'd slept with him in his guest room, and they'd shared room-service breakfast. That was a first for her. They'd spent the day at the beach, in and out of the gentle surf, and had gone to Rancho Casa again for dinner. This morning he'd taken her out to Jo Potter's farm and shown her some of the cutest little animals she'd ever seen. The goats seemed to take to him as much as Shannon did. It was clear that the goat farmer really liked Billy, and her husband seemed like a fan as well. Shannon liked Billy, too. More than she'd ever liked a guy. It might almost be love, if she wasn't careful.

He seemed to know what she wanted before she did too, in and out of bed. He was perfect for her, if she could manage to get out of her own way. She was afraid she'd ruined him somehow. It was a really good thing he was leaving at the end of the week. For him, anyway.

They sat at the beach again this afternoon, watching the sun slowly dip into the watery horizon from one of the benches lining the walk. She wore a flowered sundress that made her feel light and free, and he wore a sea-green polo over those cargo shorts she loved on him. She would miss him so much when he left.

"Hey, what's with the frown?" he asked.

"What? Oh, it's nothing."

He took her hand in his, threading his fingers through hers. "I wanted to talk to you about something."

Her heart tripped. "What?"

"I'm going back in a few days, Shannon. I want you to come with me."

Alarm trilled through her. "Why?"

"Look, baby." He angled his body, that body she knew so well now, to face her. "My future is in Cypress, and I want you in it."

Her mouth dropped open. Too late, she noticed she'd kicked off her sandals. Her toes were in the sand. *Oh, God.* "Billy, I can't."

"Can't what, exactly?"

"Can't do this." She pulled her hand out of his. "This isn't me. This relationship stuff, Billy. I suck at it."

He blinked at her, apparently confused. "You don't. You made me fall in love with you easily enough."

Now she was panicked. "Love? Oh, no." She stood, grabbing her sandals. "You can't mean that."

"Why the hell not?" He stood and gently grasped her wrist. "Why can't I love you?"

She shook her head, her hair whipping around her face. "I'm not lovable. I'm a mess-maker. I'll make a mess of this."

"Damn it, Shannon."

He stood very close to her and she caught the scent of him. Hot and fresh and tempting. She couldn't give in to the temptation, though. No way.

"Let me go," she whispered.

He dropped his hands from her like she burned him. "Is it because of me? You don't care about me?"

"I do." She was messing this up, like everything else. "I do care, but I can't go back there. My life is here now."

"Bullshit. That's just an excuse."

She welcomed the flash of anger when it came. "You

don't know me, Billy."

"The hell I don't." He raked his fingers through his hair, an expression of utter frustration on his face. "I've seen you go through guys who didn't give a shit about you, Shannon. I've seen how sweet and smart and sassy you are. I love you."

She couldn't do this. Holding her sandals in her hands, she ran toward the resort. Tears blinded her, and she didn't stop until she realized that the pavement of the parking lot was burning the soles of her feet.

"Stupid toes," she murmured, slipping her sandals back on her feet. "Stupid Billy."

But he wasn't stupid. He was sweet and kind and a great guy. He deserved so much more than her, and after he left he'd see that.

The fact that he would take her heart back with him was something she'd just have to keep to herself.

Chapter 10

Billy paced the length of his guest room, his mind churning. For what felt like the thousandth time he thought about everything Shannon had said, and hadn't said, on Sunday. She wasn't lovable? Bullshit.

It was late Tuesday afternoon, and he'd managed to stay away from the spa for nearly two days. He'd driven out to Jo Potter's again, helping her milk the goats yesterday. He'd helped her make soap today, and picked her brain about scents and formulas. She'd given him some great tips on scents, but he'd stayed away from the almond. It reminded him too much of Friday night in the big bathtub.

The goddamn sunset would come again and, like last night, it would just serve to remind him of the incredible nights he'd spent with her. Nights they'd never have again, if she had her way.

"The hell with that."

Today's visit with Jo Potter had given him an unexpected boon. It was an opportunity he'd never thought would come his way, and he'd have to be crazy not to consider it. It would mean putting his dream on hold, and that might screw up his deal with the developer up in Cypress

Corners. There were restrictions on developing that land, and owning it only to leave it vacant for an extended period of time, was very much restricted.

He sat on his bed and dropped his head into his hands. Did he want to postpone, and possible fuck up, his deal up in Central Florida? No. Did he want to lose Shannon for good? Also, no.

His senses tingled as the almond scent hit him again. His eyes fell on the diminished bar of soap set on the edge of the bathtub. He'd lathered her amazing body over and over again, caressing her every dip and curve. Indulged them both in more passion than he'd even imagined in the six long months since their first time. Passion that still made his breath quicken. At least he had a lot more of her to keep in his memory this time.

He had to consider Jo's offer, if only for his peace of mind. She'd been impressed by his degree, and had complimented his touch with the little critters. Offering him the position of second in command at the goat farm, second to only her, was very flattering. If he decided to take it, to forego his opportunity back in Cypress, it would be for one reason only. It would keep him near Shannon. It would give him time to make her see that he loved her. That she was worth anything. Hell, that she was worth everything.

"She'd see then, wouldn't she?" Who the hell knew? But he had to try.

He pulled out his phone and scrolled through his contacts. He found Jo and tapped on her name. Pacing again, he waited for her to answer.

"Hey, Billy." Her voice sounded warm and very Jo. "What's up?"

"I've been thinking about your offer."

"Yeah? Hmm. I made a wager with Ethan. Please tell me I'll be taking a cool ten bucks from him tonight?"

Billy laughed. "He bet against me?"

"Apparently he'd seen how you lit up when you talked about having your own farm. Heck, I did too."

Billy's lips thinned. He really did want his own stake. A way to prove to his uncle's memory that he was worth his trust. His inheritance.

"I can't pass up the offer to stay in Serenity Shores, Jo," he admitted.

"We'd be fortunate to have you. I can't help but guess that more than my adorable does are keeping you here. It's

Shannon, right?"

Billy blew out a breath. "Yeah. It's Shannon."

"Put your toes in the sand, did you?"

"Huh?"

"Serenity Shores, Billy. Toes in the sand, heart in your hand. It's what the locals like to say."

He found a smile. "I guess so, then."

"So when do you want to get together to go over the particulars?" she asked.

"Whenever is good for you. It won't take me long to tie up some loose ends in Cypress, and then I can come back for good."

"Okay, I'll be in touch. Let me get with Ethan and we'll all settle on a date and time."

"Sounds good."

"I'm very happy you'll be coming on board with us, Billy. See you soon."

"Yeah, see you soon."

They ended the call and Billy sat down on the bed again. That was it. He was staying. The loose ends he'd told Jo about had everything to do with the property he'd been lucky to grab, and now he was going to lose it.

"Toes in the sand, huh?" He thought about Shannon's sandals, laying on the sand beneath the bench on Sunday. She'd freaked out and grabbed them, holding them close to her chest as she'd run away from him. It hit him then. She wasn't afraid of him loving her. No. It was something even bigger than that. She was afraid of loving him.

Shannon mattered. What they had mattered. He would figure out a way to make her see that, and she would admit what he now knew.

She loved him, too.

***

Shannon clicked through Wednesday afternoon's appointments, happy to close them out. Today had been hectic, just like last Wednesday, but at least the time had flown. She'd been dragging herself through the motions since Sunday, unable to erase the memory of the shocked and saddened expression on Billy's face for more than a few minutes at a time. He loved her? Well, he thought he loved her. Still, no one had ever told her that.

"So do you want to talk about it?" Carrie asked.

Shannon looked over at her friend, seeing the concern on her face. "Nothing to talk about."

120

"Yeah, okay. Then why hasn't Billy Goat been in here the past three days?"

Shannon managed to shrug. "I don't know."

Carrie clicked her tongue. "How long is he down here for?"

"He's leaving Friday." Shannon winced. "I mean, I think that's when he's leaving."

Carrie started to say something, but turned toward the doors of the spa. Shannon looked up, tamping down her disappointment when it wasn't Billy standing in front of her. Wasn't she relieved that he hadn't been coming by? That's what she'd been telling herself, anyway.

"Hello," she said to Jo Potter. "How are you?"

"Hi, Shannon."

The smile on Jo's face looked genuine and she had a warm air about her. Shannon had noticed that right away when she'd met her out at her farm.

"What can I do for you, Jo?"

"I'm meeting my husband at Wisteria for dinner, so I thought I'd stop by and see how my soaps are moving."

"Like hotcakes," Carrie piped up. "Shannon makes sure all of the spa guests get a sample and then she sends them right in to me."

Jo grinned. "That's what I like to hear. Hey, why don't you and Billy join us for dinner, Shannon?"

"We're not…" Shannon looked from Jo to Carrie and back again. "We're not together."

Jo's brows rose. "But last night Billy said he'd put his toes in the sand."

"He did?" Carrie smirked in Shannon's direction. "Really?"

"He didn't," Shannon rushed out. "He couldn't."

Jo nodded. "He could and he did. When we talked about his new job."

"What new job?" Carrie asked.

"He didn't tell you?" Jo asked Shannon.

"No." Shannon swallowed. "Billy and I haven't talked since Sunday."

"He's coming to work for Ethan and me, Shannon. He's going to be my second-in-command."

"But what about his farm?" Shannon had to know.

"He told me he's going to tie up some loose ends, so I guess that means he's not doing that. For a while, anyway."

"No." Shannon's heart raced. "Why? Billy couldn't wait

to open that place. To build his house."

Jo's eyes rounded. "He was going to live there? I didn't know that."

"He wants what you have, Jo," Shannon said. "On a smaller scale, but something of his own."

"Hmm. That makes sense," Jo said. "He told us that he wanted to prove that he was worth the money his uncle left him."

"Oh, that's kind of sweet," Carrie said.

"Why would he give all of that up?" Shannon asked.

Jo tilted her head. "Don't you know?"

Shock rippled through Shannon. "He can't do that." She grabbed her phone, tapping on Billy's name. "I can't let him do that."

Meet me at the beach, she texted.

A few seconds ticked by. Would he answer her? They hadn't even talked since Sunday. Her phone dinged with his message, thank God.

Where?

Her heart did that flip thing.

The bench where we sat on Sunday.

When?

"When," she mused aloud.

"Now!" Carrie said. "I'll watched the desk."

"And I'll watch the shop," Jo said.

"Oh, thank you," she told them, thumbing the keys on her phone.

Ten minutes?

Okay.

She bit her lip, cradling her phone against her chest. "Yes," she whispered.

"Wait." Carrie unbuttoned the top two buttons of Shannon's blouse and fluffed her hair. "There. Just gorgeous. Right, Jo?"

"Definitely," Jo beamed. "Now get out of here."

Shannon took in a shuddering breath. "Okay. Bye."

"Good luck!" Carrie called.

Shannon managed to walk through the sumptuous lobby on her way out to the bay. The bench where she'd had her freak out three days ago wasn't far from the resort's pool, so she headed past the bar and through the lounges and tables to step out onto the sand. When she reached the bench, she saw Billy standing there. His back was to her, so she stopped and caught her breath.

He must have heard her because he turned his head, and then faced her. "Hey."

He looked worried, and so dear to her. She was the one who should be worried. She was the one who screwed up on Sunday. This was her chance to fix her mess.

"Hey." She slipped off her wedges and stepped toward him. "My toes are in the sand."

He stared at her for a beat before that beautiful smile spread across his face. "That they are."

"I love you, Billy."

He closed the distance between them and grabbed her to him. "You love me?"

She nodded, her throat tight. "I do. I'm sorry about Sunday. I freaked out."

"Yeah, you did."

"I just didn't get it, Billy. Why you love me."

He touched her cheek, stroking gently and just right. "You can't see how wonderful you are, Shannon. You're perfect for me."

"And you're perfect for me."

He crinkled his nose and flashed a bright smile, hugging her again.

"So you won't take the job with the Potters, then?" she had to know.

"How do you know about that?"

"Jo came into the spa. Don't do it, Billy. You have to build your dream. It's important to you."

He shook his head. "You're important to me. You don't want to go back with me, so I thought if I stayed in Serenity Shores you would finally realize that you love me. Seems I didn't have to wait too long."

She smiled up at him. "But Cypress is where your future is, right?" At his nod she continued. "And my future is with you."

He took a breath and brought his face to hers. "You'll come back to Cypress with me, then? For good?"

Her heart in her throat, she nodded. That balloon of want and like in her chest morphed into love, and she kissed him hard on the mouth. "Yes."

He let out a laugh and stepped back. Toeing off his Vans, he wriggled his bare feet in the sand. He kissed her now, sending warmth and want through her as she held tightly to him. Billy Harris. Hot and sweet Billy Goat. And he was all hers.

Billy saw her in a way no other guy ever had. And now she saw herself as he did. Worthy of happiness. Worthy of love. And worthy of the best guy she'd ever known.

Marion was right. It sure was fun to dip your toes in the sand and give someone your heart.

Discover other books by JoMarie DeGioia

The Secret Hearts series, including

The Courtesan Countess

The Bridgewater Brides series, including

The Heir's Treasure

The Viscount's Vixen

The Earl's Beauty

The Gentlemen Undercover series, including

A Hero and a Gentleman

The Shopgirls of Bond Street series, including

That Determined Mister Latham

The Dashing Nobles series, including

More Than Passion

Pride and Fire

Just Perfect

More Than Charming

The Cypress Corners series, including

Finding Harmony

Taming Jake

Loving Cassie

Winning Ben

Showing Jessie

Seeing Shannon

Dreaming Eli

Giving Chase

Kissing Bree

Wishing Joy

Bugging Nate

The Gifted YA Fantasy/Adventure Trilogy, including

Gifted

Braunachs of the Dell series, including

Luke's Gold

Patrick's Promise

Sexy Historical Novellas, including

In the Lady's Heart

In the Baron's Bed

In the Knight's Chamber

Connect with me online

Twitter: https://twitter.com/JoMarieDeGioia

Facebook:

https://www.facebook.com/JoMarie.DeGioia.Author

Website: www.jomariedegioia.com

About the Author

JoMarie DeGioia is a bestselling author of Historical and Contemporary Romance. She's known Mickey Mouse from the "inside," has been a copyeditor for her tiny town's newspaper, and a bookseller. She is the author of nearly 50 Romances, and writes Young Adult Fantasy/Adventure stories and Paranormal Romance too. She gets lost in DIY projects around the house and works out plot ideas during long runs. She divides her time between Central Florida and New England.